D0053276

The Iceberg
and Its
Shadow

✄ ✄

Jan Greenberg

Farrar, Straus and Giroux
NEW YORK

Siskiyou County
School Library

Copyright © 1980 by Jan Greenberg
All rights reserved
Printed in the United States of America
Published simultaneously in Canada by
McGraw-Hill Ryerson Ltd., Toronto

First printing, 1980

Grateful acknowledgment is made to Holt, Rinehart and Winston
for permission to use the poem "Steam Shovel," from
Upper Pasture by Charles Malam, copyright 1930,
renewed © 1958 by Charles Malam,
and to William Jay Smith for permission to use his poem
"The Toaster" from The Laughing Time, published by Atlantic-
Little, Brown, 1955, copyright © 1953, 1955 by William Jay Smith

Grateful acknowledgment is also made to Scholastic Magazines,
Inc., for permission to use party ideas from The Dynamite
Party Book by Linda Williams Aber,
copyright © 1978 by Linda Williams Aber.

Library of Congress Cataloging in Publication Data
Greenberg, Jan
The iceberg and its shadow.
[1. Friendship—Fiction. 2. School stories]
I. Title. PZ7.G8275Ic [Fic]
80–20060 ISBN 0–374–33624–5

For Ronnie, with love

*The Iceberg
and Its
Shadow*

1 ⁂ New Girl in Town

My best friend, Rachel Horwitz, tells me I have a fine sense of the ridiculous. What she means by that, I think, is that I always notice life's little oddities. For instance, a garden hose curled up in the grass reminds me of a sea serpent. Our principal, Dr. Munch, looks like a duck, and his laugh sounds like an owl hooting. A boy in my class, Neil Bennet, stores food in his mouth like a chipmunk, and my father snorts like a bulldog when he's mad.

In her own quiet way, Rachel doesn't miss anything, either. Only instead of telling jokes, she draws pictures. She says she's going to be another Picasso someday. I believe her, too, since she's always scribbling away on her sketch pad. From the first time we spotted each other in kindergarten, we've been a self-appointed team, dedicated to furthering the intellectual and social scene at Skokie Elementary School.

One of our best schemes was to start a school newspaper: *The Skokie Scuttlebutt*. She'd do cartoons; I'd write articles. Our teacher, Mrs. Trilling, set aside an hour one Monday morning for a planning session.

"You do the talking, Anabeth," Rachel whispered. "You're good at that." Then she settled back and began doodling. Totally absorbed in her design of a two-footed Tyrannosaurus, she didn't seem to be listening while I explained our idea to the other kids. Rachel's all wrapped up in a new plan that involves painting what she calls the corporate giant on the outside wall of her dad's office building. She claims she needs to pattern the eighteen-foot dinosaur mural exactly to scale and that takes concentration. Lately, she's more interested in her protractor, graph paper, and Prisma color pencils than in our newspaper, or playing after school, or even gossiping on the phone. I found myself trying to sell our newspaper plan to the rest of the group all by myself.

"We'll write feature stories about each class with headlines like the 'Skokie School Spotlight' or 'V.I.P. of the Month.' "

"What about a humor section and a monthly editorial?" suggested Neil. "I think this establishment needs a longer lunch hour, one o'clock dismissal, and a three-month school year."

"Speaking of humor," said Billy Moran, "what's the difference between a girl and an umbrella?"

"You can shut an umbrella up," replied Neil.

The boys broke up into rowdy laughter.

Carolyn Turner put her index fingers to her lips and let out a huge wolf whistle. That shut EVERYONE up. I can always count on Carolyn and her sidekick, Tracy Silversmith, to back me up. Tracy, who is a wisp, dainty, and bashful, dissolves into embarrassed giggles whenever she has to stand up in front of the class; while Carolyn, who has a Perma-Prest memory, can learn twenty-five spelling words in thirty seconds and loves a captive audience. She did a report on "Monks and Monasteries" for Medieval Mirth Day that went on for an hour before Mrs. Trilling politely told her to sit down.

Tracy goes to Dr. Klein for allergy shots and Carolyn says the nurse has to chase Tracy around the office until she pretends to faint on the waiting-room floor. Once Tracy slept over and woke up crying in the middle of the night. Mrs. Silversmith came to get her in a red flannel night-gown and pink plastic curlers. Tracy also sets her alarm for 8:45 and then sleeps right through 9:00 attendance every day. She sticks to Carolyn like glue and Carolyn has been sticking close to me ever since she moved to Skokie. The older girls made fun of her Southern drawl and her homemade dresses (the kind old-fashioned dolls wear—long and plaid with white aprons) but I was always nice to her. Now Carolyn doesn't say "y'all" or "ha" instead of "hi" any more, and she wears jeans like the rest of us. But I think somewhere deep inside she still believes she's an outcast from Vidalia, Georgia. She covers it up by making more noise than a cluster of crows.

"We'll have to make a list of all the sections and staff positions first," she blared, flapping her arms.

"Who's going to be managing editor?" asked Neil.

"I think Anabeth should be." Tracy giggled. "Who else could come up with a word like 'scuttlebutt'?"

Even though Rachel was sitting there, spaced-out, lost in her network of grids and diagrams, I suggested that

5

she be my co-editor. Rachel always prompts my most creative attempts. Carolyn's shoulders slumped when I didn't choose her, but she knew the paper had been Rachel's idea as much as mine.

"Why don't you write a gossip column," I suggested, "or, 'Helpful Hints for Skipping School.' " Carolyn nodded but didn't look convinced.

For some reason, my heart just wasn't into this new project. I didn't feel very excited even after the group agreed unanimously to initiate *The Skokie Scuttlebutt*. Normally, I would have been helping Carolyn with her lists, jotting down notes, chattering away, but instead I felt antsy, eager for the bell to ring for gym. These were the last few months of my last year at Skokie Elementary School. I've been going to the same place with the same people since I was six. I looked around the room. Some of the boys were staring at me—as usual. Rachel was drawing—as usual. Tracy and Carolyn were whispering— as usual. Mrs. Trilling was smiling about my latest brainstorm—as usual. It all felt too much like the usual.

As we were delegating jobs, a hush fell over the classroom. At first there was a drop in the noise level and gradually no more rustling of papers or banging of books. I looked up. Standing with her legs apart and her hands on her hips, a tall, hefty girl posed at the doorway and surveyed the scene. Flashy in her shiny red bomber jacket and silver-studded jeans, she looked us over, almost daring someone to look away or try to ignore her. She was hardly a breath of fresh air with her curled-lip smirk and unkempt black hair, but nevertheless, there was an aura of excitement about her, a hint of danger. She definitely

6

intended to cause a stir, and I was definitely in the mood for one. Instead of pussyfooting around quietly like most new kids do, she swaggered over to Mrs. Trilling's desk and shoved a crumpled note in her face.

"Ah, yes. Mindy Gottfried," said Mrs. Trilling, smiling at her warmly. "We're so happy to have you with us. Let me introduce you to the class." She started to put her arm around Mindy, who ducked and chose not to smile back. Mindy did manage a gruff, halfhearted hello in our direction. Even the boys acted shy when they told her their names. Mindy's eyes flicked back and forth suspiciously. I could tell she was sizing us up, trying to figure out where she fit in. She was like a wild bird in an aviary of canaries. She seemed perched there, ready to swoop.

"Anabeth," said Mrs. Trilling, "since you're student-council president, why don't you show Mindy around and help her get settled." I felt proud to be singled out. Strangely, I wanted Mindy to know who I was right away.

We cruised through the library without stopping. Reading was not high on Mindy's list of favorite pastimes. When I mentioned that I wanted to win the Reading Circle Award for finishing the most books, she said, "Big thrill."

"I like your jeans," I told her as she poked her head in the science lab and right back out again.

"I bought them on Oak Street in Chicago," she said with more enthusiasm.

I knew that's where people shop for far-out clothes. My mother prefers Marshall Field's because she likes shopping for everything in one place and also because that's where she's been buying what she calls "sturdy, no-

nonsense clothes" for years. Mindy checked out my khaki pants and holey ski sweater as if to say "What's with that?" I'll bet she used to collect Barbie Doll clothes.

"I know how to stick in the studs if you want me to help you make a pair." Her tone was friendly, almost eager, so I nodded and smiled.

We passed the art and music rooms, the special reading nook, and the display cases in record time. But Mindy perked up when we reached the lunchroom.

"I hope the food's not rotten here. We had a great cafeteria at my old school—hamburgers and hot dogs every day."

I decided not to tell her about the prepackaged plate lunches: mushy corn and meat loaf on Mondays, degenerating to fish sticks and peas on Fridays.

"You better plan on bringing your own," I said.

Mindy was clearly on familiar territory in the gym. She proceeded to do three back flips and a handstand on the mats, and swing from the rings like Tarzan in the jungle. None of the boys can move that quickly.

"Hot stuff," remarked old Macho Michaels, the gym teacher, who thinks girls and sports are as incompatible as monkeys and mathematics.

"That's nothing," said Mindy, staring him down. I was beginning to enjoy her gutsy "no one can mess with me" attitude. I had never talked back to a teacher before.

When we passed the Early Childhood Center, all the little ones started yelling, "Hi, Anabeth," and tagging after us.

"Everyone here knows your name," said Mindy. "That's cool."

8

"Oh, it's a small school," I said modestly, but I was glad she was impressed.

Right away, Mindy moved her desk next to mine and Rachel's. Rachel was too busy trying to pass D section in our math workbook to notice. But I could tell by the way they edged their desks up to ours and hung on Mindy's every word that Carolyn and Tracy were fascinated. She talked non-stop for the rest of the day. She told us she hates her father and her big sister, Lorna, but her brother, Tim, is all right. "He's the only one in the house who doesn't yell at me. The rest of them are nuts. My mother's in a bad mood 'cause she had to sell our house and move to Skokie after the divorce." Tracy, Carolyn, and I looked at each other. Sometimes we complain about our families, but not the way Mindy did. She didn't care what she said about them.

"Come over after school," she told me. "You'll see what I mean."

On my way home I decided that our first feature story would be about Mindy. I couldn't wait to go over to her place. I wanted to sniff out some facts for my article. I have a nose for detail.

Today my nose detected a pungent, smoky odor wafting down the street when I turned the corner onto my lane. I quickened my pace. An aroma like that could be coming only from one place—my house.

"Why does the kitchen smell like rotten eggs?" I shouted to Mother as I climbed through the kitchen window. The back door's been stuck for months because Mother says our house is too old and big for her to worry about technicalities.

"I burned my lunch," she said absently, her head bent over her usual kind of book—large, fat, with titles like *Snap, Crackle, and Popular Culture*. Mother went back to college last fall, but she's not sure yet what she wants to do with the rest of her life. Meanwhile, she pores over her books, which are cluttered on tables, chairs, at counters, in corners, on stairways and window seats. A book was balanced precariously on top of the icebox.

"Hard-boiled eggs again, huh?" I sniffed.

"Hmmmm," she said, which meant she wasn't paying attention. "Anabeth, listen to this: 'We cannot escape the future by turning our backs on it.' " Then she turned her back on me and continued reading. I looked up at the ceiling. There was egg splattered all over the chandelier.

"You let the eggs boil too long again, didn't you?" Mother has a passion for hard-boiled eggs and avocados mushed up with vinegar. She never throws away the pits, so we have thirty-five avocado plants straggling long and spindly all over the house.

"Well," she said, "I was preoccupied with this chapter on self-expression. I'll drag the ladder up from the basement later and clean it up. Anyway, if you think this smells bad, go up to the second floor. I accidentally knocked over a bottle of perfume and decided to use it to mop all the floors. The combination of Norell and burned eggs is devastating." She chortled, tickled by her own disorder.

"I'm allergic to that stuff," I groaned. "Now I'll be sneezing all night."

"What's done is done," she said. That's a favorite expression of hers, along with "Haste makes waste" and

"Better late than never." Then came the familiar "How was school today?" floating up from between the pages of her book.

"Nothing much happened except that we have a new girl in the class. Her name's Mindy Gottfried, and her family moved to an apartment on Davenport Drive since her parents are getting a divorce."

"Well, you'll have to invite her over. I'm sure she's going through a rough transition period." Mother just memorized a long list of rough transition periods for her psychology class.

The phone started ringing the way it does every day at 3:30, because all the girls call to make plans. Mother tells me I'm the social director. But I was curious about Mindy's family, so I told them I was busy. After I threw my knapsack on the floor in my room, I left the house holding my nose and coughing, but Mother didn't even notice.

The Gottfrieds' apartment was small and crowded with glass tables and low couches, covered in material that was supposed to look like suede. The place had the air of a temporary dwelling. Mrs. Gottfried was on the phone when I walked in. "Listen, Carl," she was saying in the kind of tone my mother uses when she talks to my dad's sister, Helen, "I don't want you coming around here except on your regular visiting days. I'm not your wife any more." Then she banged down the receiver and muttered, "Damn," under her breath. When she turned around and saw me standing there, her face became all cheery and full of smiles.

"Oh, you must be Mindy's new little friend," she said

Siskiyou County
School Library

in a voice that could be poured over pancakes. She was at least six feet tall and so skinny that her hipbones stood out. Her black hair hung down to her waist and she had the longest red fingernails I'd ever seen.

"Call me Natasha," she said sweetly. Dragon Lady was more fitting. Then, with her other voice, which sounded something like the roar of a vacuum cleaner, she yelled, "Tim, get in here and help me unpack. Do I have to do everything around here?"

"Just shut up. I'm coming" was the muffled reply from the back of their apartment. I could also hear Mindy yelling and another voice rasping, "You little twerp! You stupid hockey puck!" That had to be Lorna, I decided. She sounded like bad news. The Gottfried residence promised some new excitement in my life. At our house the cardinal rule is that everyone "dialogues like sane, intelligent human beings"—in other words, we're not supposed to call each other bad names or raise our voices.

I wandered into the back hall and bumped right into Lorna, who was storming out of the bedroom. She was a carbon copy of Natasha, except that her hair was red and her fingernails were painted black. She didn't even say excuse me.

Mindy was curled up on the bed with a sneer of satisfaction on her face.

"I unpacked first, so Lorna has to use the closet in the hall. She's furious 'cause when we lived in Highland Park, she had her own bedroom and now she has to share it with me.

"We lived in a big house there," she continued, "but

when Mom and Dad were divorced, Dad made us move to this stupid apartment. Maybe my mother will find a rich husband, although you never can tell about her." Mindy accented "her" with a twisted frown.

"Oh" was all I could think of to say. I'd never heard anyone talk that way before. Mindy sounded as if she not only disapproved of her mother but also of the apartment. And I wondered what she'd say when she saw my house with its jumble of rooms, crisscrossing hallways, and stone fireplaces.

"Hey, let's go up to the playground," said Mindy. "That's where everyone hangs out, isn't it?"

I wanted to stick around the apartment and see what would happen next, but I could tell that Mindy wasn't in the mood for another disagreement.

"Rachel's your best friend, isn't she?" she queried in a knowing fashion as we trudged up the big hill toward school.

"I guess so," I muttered. For some reason I didn't feel right talking about Rachel with Mindy.

"She's awfully quiet," said Mindy. "Someone like that can't be much fun."

It's true that Rachel's quiet—especially at school, because she's so studious, but we always find a lot to talk about.

As we turned the corner, Neil Bennet leaped down from the branch of a tree. I think he has a crush on me. He's always calling on the phone and tagging after me during recess. But sometimes he gets overly excited and I have to tell him to cut it out.

> *"Anabeth, Anabeth, Anabeth Blair,*
> *She still sleeps with her teddy bear,"*

he sang. He likes to make up silly poems for me.

"Very cute, Neil," I said. He sneaked up behind me and pulled my ponytail. It didn't hurt, but I yelled, "Ouch!" With that, Mindy gave him a karate chop and kicked him in the shins. He toppled over on the grass and looked up at her with an amazed expression. She stood there scowling, with her hands on her hips. "That'll teach you to mess around with my friend," she said. "All the boys hang around you, don't they? But Neil acts the dopiest."

"Listen, Mindy," I told her, as Neil dashed off, "it's just a game we play. Really nothing to get so upset about." There are times when I want to give Neil a clunk, too, but I never would. I can handle him in my own way.

"I just like to stick up for my best friends," she said, as she leaped over the fence that surrounds the schoolyard. I wanted to tell her that I could take care of myself, but instead I followed behind her. She was so tough and sure of herself that I couldn't find the words to disagree.

Within twenty minutes, Mindy had organized the whole playground into a game of kickball. "I'll be captain of the A team," she said.

I started to move over the line to choose the B team.

"Anabeth," Mindy called, "stick with me. I want you on my team. I know we can beat them."

"The teams should be even," I told her. It's not fair if one side is much better than the other. Even when I'm not captain, I'm usually chosen first. I knew the game would be more fun if I stayed on the other team, but Mindy kept jumping up and down saying, "Please, please," and grabbing my arm. She was so insistent that I told Laurie James to go ahead and be captain.

"Tell me who the good players are so we can have the best team," Mindy demanded. I felt disloyal whispering about the others. When Mindy skipped over Carolyn and Tracy, I knew I shouldn't have told her they score an absolute zero when it comes to kickball. Carolyn's so clumsy, she trips over the ball; Tracy flits around the field like Tinkerbell. I usually pick them just because we're good friends. After all, it's only a game. Naturally, our team started scoring right away. Not much of a contest!

But Mindy was jubilant. "See, I told you," she said.

It was dark when I finally said I had to go home.

"We have dinner at seven o'clock every night," I told Mindy, "and I can't be late."

"Suit yourself," she said in a way that meant that she could probably stay out as long as she wanted to. "Hey, Carolyn," she called, "want to come over and see my hamster?"

Carolyn, pleased by Mindy's attention, broke out in a big smile and they clomped away together.

At home, Mother was standing at the stove stirring spaghetti sauce with one hand and writing in a notebook with the other. She was staring intently at a large bowl containing three goldfish.

"Where and why did you buy goldfish?" I asked, shocked. In the last five years, the Blair family has gone through three birds, one turtle, two gerbils, and a dozen fish of assorted shapes and colors. By "gone through," I mean that due to illness or just plain neglect, all the little creatures have died untimely deaths, which caused Mother to decree "No more pets in this household." Therefore, the arrival of three goldfish came as a great surprise.

"I had to," she declared rather sheepishly.

"Why?"

"I have to observe and write a naturalistic study on a subhuman species for my research class," she answered.

"But goldfish are so dull," I said. "Why didn't you pick something more exotic like a mongoose or even a double-wattled cassawary. That's the meanest animal in the zoo," I added, smug about my knowledge.

"I hardly have time to go to the zoo every day," she retorted. "Besides, with our record, Mrs. Rumplemeyer at the pet store wouldn't sell me anything else."

"Not to mention the fact that you don't know what else to do with that three-gallon bowl from the last batch," added my older sister, Jill, who was sprawled out at the counter doing her homework. Jill is fifteen and has an IQ of 160, which means that she can memorize anything she reads in about two minutes flat. She's a walking encyclopedia of famous quotations. She's collecting them for a book entitled *Quips to Bridge the Generation Gap*. Sometimes I think it's hard on my mother, because Jill has already read all the same books she has and more. And she has a saying for everything. For example, when Mother criticized Jill for wearing her "Nobody's Perfect" T-shirt three days in a row, Jill said, " 'Thou shalt not belittle your child.' Fitzhugh Dodson."

That stumped my mother, who had never even heard

of Fitzhugh Dodson. Sometimes I wonder if Jill makes up some of her quotations.

"I'm calling my paper 'A Fish Tale.'"

"Very clever," Jill said.

"I'll leave this notebook on the counter, so if you happen to notice the fish doing anything unusual, just write it down for me," Mother continued, ignoring Jill's sarcasm.

Jill and I groaned simultaneously just as my dad walked through the front door.

"Spaghetti again," he said, sniffing the pot as he reached down to kiss Mother. "Or are we having goldfish?" Mother screwed up her nose at him and he laughed. They're always teasing each other. "Good Lord!" he said. "What's that other smell?"

"Just a small mishap," said Mother.

We finally sat down for dinner—burned spaghetti sauce, soggy pasta, and a salad without dressing.

"I forgot to go to the grocery store today," explained Mother.

"Memory loss is the first sign of senility," said Jill.

"Who said that?" I asked.

"Me," replied Jill. "'I often quote myself. It adds spice to my conversation.' George Bernard Shaw."

I choked on a noodle.

"The food here is so tasteless you could eat a meal of it, belch, and it wouldn't remind you of anything," quipped Jill. We both howled.

"There they go, picking on me again," said Mother.

"So what's new?" asked Dad, to divert our attention.

"We have a new girl in our class," said Jill. "She transferred in the middle of the semester from Highland Park High because her parents split up."

"Is she tall with long, red hair?" I asked.

"That's her," said Jill. "She's already managed to have every boy in the sophomore class following her around. But when she opens her mouth, she sounds like a . . ."

"Vacuum cleaner," I offered, remembering Dragon Lady and Mother's expression: "An acorn doesn't fall far from the tree."

"Right again. How do you know her?"

"Her sister Mindy's in my class and I went over there today." My dad would have been horrified by the Gottfrieds, and Jill gave me one of her disapproving sniffs, so I didn't elaborate.

"Sounds like they've already made quite an impression," remarked Dad, and then he began spouting off about his favorite topics—the Dow Jones averages and what's wrong with the economy.

2 ❧ "If I were a Jell-Ospider..."

Friday morning at school, our teacher, Mrs. Trilling, assigned a new project. "Study an insect, mammal, or fish. Write a report and if possible develop an activity around your project that the rest of the class can take part in."

"When is it due?" asked Rachel.

"Let's see," said Mrs. Trilling. "Today's the third of April; so you have six weeks."

Mindy raised her hand. "How long does it have to be?"

"That's up to you, but I hope it will include at least three or four weeks of journal entries." Then she handed out a sheet that explained the rules. I like Mrs. Trilling because she always lets us know from the beginning what she expects. Some teachers make assignments and then tell you to do the work over again, even if they haven't made their directions clear.

"I'm going to do mine on my hamster, Murgatroyd," said Mindy.

"My mother just bought some goldfish, so maybe I'll observe them."

"Goldfish are so dumb and boring," said Mindy.

"That's what you think," I retorted. But inside, I started having doubts again. Maybe Mindy was right. She sounded so positive that I began to wonder if I shouldn't abandon Mother's fish in favor of a guinea pig or a rabbit.

Rachel said, "If I know Anabeth, they won't be boring for long."

I smiled at her gratefully.

Mrs. Trilling was passing out packets of blue cards. Every card had a noun on it, like donkey, pineapple, or telephone. "We're going to play a word game this morning," she said. "Each person put two cards together to form a new word. Just play around with them until you find a combination that you like."

Rachel, Mindy, and I found so many unusual combinations that we wrote a list.

Buffalocloud
Zippertree
Battoes
Moondragon
Pocketwitch
Grasshoppershoes
Jell-Ospider

"Now," said Mrs. Trilling, "picture the word in your mind. Does anyone have a word they want to share with us?"

20

"Jell-Ospider," I called out. Some of the boys hooted.

"Very interesting," said Mrs. Trilling. "What does it look like?"

"Like a slimy, slithery octopus, only small as a spider. It tastes like strawberry Jell-O with marshmallows floating around inside."

"Can you see through it?" asked Carolyn.

"Yes." I was really getting into this. I wanted to make sure the class could picture a Jell-Ospider the way I did.

"Show us how it moves," called out Billy Moran.

There was a dead silence as I stood up and stared around the room. Mrs. Trilling gave me a smile of encouragement. I scrunched up like a spider but started shaking and rippling around. Some of the others clapped and so did Mrs. Trilling. Soon everyone in the class, except Mindy, jumped up and started Jell-Ospidering all over the room. When we finally calmed down and went back to our seats, Mindy yelled out, "I've got one. Toadeye."

"All right," said Mrs. Trilling. "What does a toadeye sound like?"

The whole class started saying "*Rrr ribbet ribbet.*"

"What does it smell like?"

"Sort of clammy like a polluted pond," said Mindy. The boys snorted and held their noses.

"Do any of the rest of you have any questions?" No one responded.

"This may be your last chance to find out about a toadeye," coaxed Mrs. Trilling.

"What does it look like?" asked Rachel.

Mindy hesitated and then she said in a deliberately loud voice, "Sort of like you." Everyone laughed except

Rachel, and when I saw Rachel grimace, I stifled my own nervous giggle. It's true that Rachel's eyes bulge out a little bit, but why did Mindy have to bring that up.

Mrs. Trilling brought the class back to order and told us to write poems about our new word pictures. Mine went like this:

If I were a Jell-Ospider like a rubbery star,
I would slip and slide through the night,
Reach out with my arms and light up the world.

"That doesn't rhyme," said Mindy.

"Poems don't have to," Rachel said.

After the activity, Rachel moved her desk away from ours to a corner near Mrs. Trilling. She started drawing furiously in the sketchbook she keeps in her desk. "I can't get any work done with Mindy blabbing all the time," she told me.

"Suit yourself," I said. I hate it when my friends don't get along. Just because Rachel didn't like Mindy, she didn't have to desert me. And then there was Mindy, who must stay up nights thinking of insulting remarks to make to Rachel even though she knows Rachel is sensitive. I should have told Mindy to ask Rachel to move back, but after they glowered at each other across the room, I decided to let them fight it out without me.

Mindy walked halfway home from school with me and we decided to go to the movies later. "There's an R-rated at the Bijou," she said.

"I'm not allowed to go to those."

"Just tell your parents that you're going to see the one next door. It's an old Walt Disney movie. They'll never know the difference. And see if your mom can drive both ways. Natasha has a hot date tonight." Then she was galloping off down the street, her wild black mane of hair flying out like streamers behind her.

Mother wasn't home, but next to the fishbowl was a manual, *Enjoy Your Goldfish*, a bottle of instant water regulator pills, and a box of fish flakes. In the notebook she had written: "All the silly fish do is swim round and round in circles for hours."

I remember the time she gave me a parakeet for Christmas. I didn't want a bird, but I made an effort to take care of the scraggly blue thing until one day I just forgot. The bird was dead for three days in its cage before anyone even noticed. Jill flushed it down the toilet before Dad came home from the office. She knew how guilty I felt, because she once had some gerbils that she put down in the basement to mate. The book said they needed a dark, cool place. Then she forgot about them, and somehow the gerbils escaped and were never seen again. She's certain that when she goes down there and hears scuffling noises the gerbils are still living somewhere behind the baseboards.

Determined not to let history repeat itself, I opened the goldfish manual. "If treated properly," it read, "you can expect your new pet to live up to two years." After I studied the manual for a while, I looked up goldfish in the *World Book Encyclopedia*. "*Carassius auratus*, the Latin name for goldfish, was domesticated by the Chinese at least as early as the Sung Dynasty." I began taking notes. After all, a good research paper had to have facts. I would have to explain to Mother how to write a report. It was clear that she was a little rusty on the subject. I discovered there were at least 125 varieties of goldfish. We had one fantail, which I named Goldy, a black telescope fish with protruding eyes that I called Goggles, and Shabunkin, a dappled single-tailed fish with short fins. I approved of Mother's choices. I watched them circling for such a long time that I felt almost hypnotized. The shrill ring of the phone startled me. It was Rachel.

"Are you coming over tonight?" Almost every Friday night we do something together. Then I remembered I had made plans with Mindy.

"I think I'm going to the movies. Want to come along?"

There was a long pause. Then she said very crisply, "If it's with Mindy, I'll pass."

"Mindy's new in Skokie," I said. "I'm just trying to be friendly."

"Well, she seems to be doing fine without me."

"Rachel, you don't have to be so stubborn. I want you to come." I knew Rachel was feeling jealous of Mindy, but I didn't want to ruin my plans because of that. Rachel has a stubborn streak. When she makes up her mind, she won't back down.

"I'll see you around." Then she hung up.

"Well, if that's the way you want to be," I muttered to the dial tone, but I felt terrible, caught in the middle. And I knew from experience that when Rachel gets upset, she retreats. She can sit at home and draw pictures for hours without getting bored. Not me. I have to be busy all the time. My family is always asking me what I'm doing on the weekends, and if I say nothing, they look at me almost accusingly. Maybe it's because Jill has so many friends and activities at school that she's hardly ever home. My father never sits still for a minute. He's either playing tennis, jogging, or working. And since Mother went back to school, she's busy, too. "Be active" is another one of the Blairs' cardinal rules.

I once heard that watching fish is relaxing. Dad's always telling me to calm down and not act so hyper, but he's as energetic as I am. If I were one of those goldfish, I'd jump right out of the bowl.

Mother agreed to cart us over to the Bijou. "I've always loved *Peter Pan*," she said to Mindy. "I have half a mind to come along with you."

Mindy nudged me with her elbow but gave Mother an angelic smile.

"That's okay, Mother," I said quickly. I was feeling bad already.

"Children under seventeen are not admitted without an adult," said the lady at the box office in a bored tone.

Mindy stood up very tall and said in a haughty "how dare you" voice, "I've been seventeen for six months." The lady shrugged. Mindy quickly paid for two tickets and we scrambled inside. It wasn't until the lights dimmed and I was settled in my seat that the butterflies in my stomach went away.

"Have you ever seen an R-rated film?" I asked Mindy.

"Sure, lots of times. They're really nothing. Natasha even takes us to X-rated films."

There was a little boy about two years old sitting

with his mother right in front of us. As soon as the movie started, he howled, "I wanna go home." I didn't blame him.

In the first five minutes, three people were shot and I counted fourteen four-letter words. The narrative was hard to follow because there wasn't one. Just a lot of shouting during the violent scenes and moaning during the sex ones. At first, Mindy was wide-eyed. I found the movie tedious from the credits on. There wasn't one likable person in the whole story. So I sat there and thought about Mindy's performance at the ticket counter. I had figured the lady would call the manager and he'd reroute us to *Peter Pan.* But Mindy pulled her trick off with style while I ducked behind her. She strutted in as if she'd just won the Academy Award. Yet she doesn't care about winning good grades or pleasing her parents—not the same way I do. Sometimes I wish I didn't care so much. But for sure Mindy likes to cause a disturbance, to be the center of attention, to be on top. I'll bet she's like a bulldozer when she wants something, and I wouldn't want to be in her way.

"Call your mother and tell her to pick us up a few minutes later so we can go across the street to the drugstore." Mindy has a short attention span even at R-rated movies.

"I don't think she'll like that idea," I said. "Let's go in front now and wait for her. If she sees us coming out of here, she'll have a conniption fit."

As we squeezed by the couple next to us, Mindy accidentally-on-purpose knocked their box of popcorn over, making a loud crunching noise under our feet. Popcorn was flying everywhere. We both started giggling and made a beeline for the exit. Mother was already waiting. She turned around when we climbed into the back seat.

Mindy said very quickly, "*Peter Pan* was sold out so we saw *Big Dan and the Turk* instead. It was so awful we left early."

If Mindy thought my mother, the human lie detector, would fall for that one, she was in for a big shock. Mother cleared her throat, raised her eyebrows, but restrained herself from commenting. I hunched down in the corner and elbowed Mindy in a lame attempt to keep her quiet, but she continued.

"I'm really disappointed. Maybe I'll come back and see *Peter Pan* tomorrow night."

After we dropped Mindy off, Mother asked, "Don't you usually do something with Rachel on Friday nights?"

"She didn't want to come," I mumbled.

"Well," said Mother, "it's nice to make a new friend, but don't forget about your old ones in the process. And tell me next time you want to go to an R-rated movie."

3 ❧ Carl's Chili con Carne Cockamamie

Saturday morning, I told Jill I was going over to Rumplemeyer's Pet Store. Referring to Mrs. Rumplemeyer, who keeps at least twenty dogs there, Jill said, " 'I have always thought of a dog lover as a dog that was in love with another dog.' James Thurber."

"Very funny," I said, climbing out the kitchen window. "Tell Mother to get this stupid door fixed today."

I love Mrs. Rumplemeyer's Pet Store, even though I don't love Mrs. Rumplemeyer. Whenever she looks at me, I know she's thinking to herself, There's one of those Blairs again. Fish take one look at them and drop dead. Mother says she used to go to that pet store when she was a little girl. So I imagine that Mrs. Rumplemeyer must be at least a hundred years old. She looks just like her cat, Methuselah, small and frail. She even has whiskers. She slants her eyes and arches her back whenever kids in the neighborhood tease her parrot, Calypso, who sits perched in a large gold cage in back of the shop. Calypso says two sentences: "Get outta here" and "Who cares?" He also screeches constantly.

The fish tanks continuously hum; the Shih Tzu puppies whimper and yelp, and the whole place smells like a giant bag of Ken-L-Ration. There's nothing that Mrs. Rumplemeyer doesn't stock for pets: leashes, kitty litter, Milk-Bones, tick spray, and every size cage imaginable, stacked carelessly in corners. I love to poke around the store, but because of our high pet mortality rate, I try to keep a low profile. When Mrs. Rumplemeyer comes up one aisle, I edge down the opposite one.

Despite her negative attitude toward me, I wanted to interview Mrs. Rumplemeyer for my report. She was behind the counter adding up some figures. She knew I was standing there, but didn't look up. "So you're back to fish again," she finally said. "Are they still alive?"

"Well, that's what I wanted to talk to you about," I started, very assertively.

She looked up at me with slanty eyes.

"You see, I'm writing this report for school and I thought you might be able to give me some information . . . uh, based on your long experience," I gulped out.

"What do you need to know? I'm very busy today, but I'll try to answer your questions."

I had brought along my loose-leaf notebook, so I thought I looked very professional.

"How do you convince a customer that the fish are healthy when they buy them from you?" I began.

"They take my word for it," she said huffily.

"Where do you get your fish?" I continued, ignoring her lack of enthusiasm.

"From reliable dealers. However, they're overseas distributors, so I have to accept what they send, sight unseen." Then she showed me a pale-pink, lusterless-looking fish who was jerking around in the fish tank. The rest of the goldfish were swimming smoothly. "That little fellow's just about had it." She removed the sick one with a small net and deposited him in a separate tank. "If one of your fish begins lying motionless for long periods of time at the bottom of the bowl or goes into convulsions, there's not much you can do." I could tell she was warming to the subject. There was hope for me and Mrs. Rumplemeyer after all.

"Despite the fact that there are many fancy varieties of tropical fish, I still sell more goldfish than any other kind. By the way, do you have anything besides the fish in your bowl?"

"Well, I'm thinking of putting in some of the shells I found on the beach in Florida."

"Don't you dare do that!" She arched her back again. "Sharp edges are dangerous for the bubble-eyed fish. You do need some gravel, though." Then she gave me a whole bag, free, and a plant called a bushy Sagittaria.

"The fish sometimes like to hide in the greenery or just nibble on the leaves." I'll bet she knows all there is to know about her birds and fish. She has special names for them, and some of the birds eat right out of her hand. I think she likes them better than people. She must be able to tell I'm a serious customer this time, I told myself as I collected my parcels and headed for the door. Her regard for animals was contagious. Now I was eager to go home and fix up the goldfish bowl.

"Whatever you do, don't stick your fingers in the water," she called after me. "That makes the fish nervous."

The bushy Sagittaria spread itself like a green squid in the bowl. It took about an hour for the gravel to settle to the bottom. I put Goldy, Goggles, and Shabunkin in a milk carton filled with water while I was organizing their new setting. I hoped Mother wouldn't mind my decorations. Then I noticed her notebook entry for the day.

> This reminds me of a cartoon that appeared in last week's *New Yorker*, picturing two goldfish in a bowl. One said to the other, "Shall we take one more spin around before we turn in?" The point is that these fish lead monotonous lives. They make being a housewife look glamorous.

Maybe this project will bring Mother back to the kitchen and out of the books, so we can have a decent meal around here.

At five-thirty, Mindy called, "Where were you this morning?"

"Just up to the pet store," I replied.

"Who with?"

"Myself." What was this, the third degree? I'd only known Mindy a few days and already she acted as if I should check with her before I made any other plans.

"Well," she said rather accusingly, "I've been trying to reach you all day. Natasha went away for the weekend and Dad's coming over to fix dinner. Want to come?"

I was curious about Mindy's dad, too, so I left Mother a note and rode my bike over to the Gottfrieds'.

Mindy's dad, Carl, was standing in the kitchen looking exasperated. Lorna, who towered over him, was saying, "What did you have to come over for? We can take care of ourselves."

Carl was sporting a Hawaiian shirt and patchwork plaid trousers. Not only didn't the summer outfit match, but it was forty degrees outside. He was bald on the top except for one tuft of red hair. But I liked the sound of his voice when he said to Lorna, "I know you can take care of yourself, but I miss you and welcome the opportunity to spend some time here."

"Well, I'm going out after dinner, so don't expect me to stick around and keep you company." She flounced out of the room, leaving Mr. Gottfried standing there like a spanked puppy. He brightened when he saw Mindy. She gave him a snarl, too. I couldn't understand why they didn't like him. He seemed so nice and kind of lonely, too. I decided to ask Mindy about him later.

"Help me set the table," he said to her. "I'm going to whip up a batch of my famous tacos and chili."

"This is my friend Anabeth," said Mindy, "and we're busy."

"That's all right," I said. "I'll be glad to help." Mindy shot me a poisoned-dart look, but I ignored her.

Tim strolled in. He was tall with red curly hair and freckles. Mindy says he's the best athlete in the high school. Jill doesn't know who he is. "Hey, Dad," he said.

Carl hugged him. "How's it going, son?"

"All right, I guess . . . even though I have to listen to

a bunch of cackling females all the time." He ruffled Mindy's hair.

"Can you stay for supper?" Carl was tying on a frilly apron.

"Sorry, Dad, I have baseball practice. Why don't you come over to the field later?"

"Great," said Mr. Gottfried. "You can come back to my place for a beer."

I could tell that he and Tim got along fine.

Within an hour, Carl served up the most delicious batch of tacos I've ever tasted. The shells were hot and crispy, filled with spicy meat, melted cheese, and shredded lettuce. The chili was even better, with chunks of beef, his homemade tomato sauce, and green peppers. He put an extra bowl of cheddar cheese on the table.

"It's the peppers that do the trick," he said proudly. "I also use cinnamon."

"Maybe you'll give my mother the recipe," I said. "She needs some inspiration."

"Sorry, there is a secret ingredient which I can't divulge yet. I'm entering the Skokie, Illinois, annual chili cook-off, and I plan to win."

"You're forty-two," snapped Lorna. "Don't you think you're a little old for chili contests?"

"Now you're sounding just like your mother," Carl said.

"Well, I think it's ridiculous! The only people who enter chili contests must be absolute nerds."

"If I win," said Carl, ignoring her, "they're going to add my chili to the menu at the Rainbow Inn. Carl's Chili con Carne Cockamamie."

"Dad's been entering chili contests for years," explained Mindy in a disgusted tone. "Problem is, he never wins."

"I once took the judges out to lunch at a cook-off in Carbondale, Illinois, and that didn't even help." Carl laughed. "But this time I know I'm going to win first place."

"Well, good luck," I said. "I think your chili's the greatest."

Then Mindy whispered, "Don't encourage him," and dragged me away from the table.

Carl and Lorna were left arguing over who was going to do the dishes.

4 ≈ The Great Fish-Tale Experiment

First period Monday morning, Mrs. Trilling divided us up in groups of four and handed each group a large brown paper bag tied with string.

"I'll bet it's another one of her artsy-craftsy projects," said Mindy under her breath.

I didn't answer. I think Mrs. Trilling's art projects are fun. I can tell that our principal isn't fond of them either, because I once heard him tell Mrs. Trilling to concentrate on the basic skills instead of always doing plays and drawing pictures.

Mrs. Trilling said to him, "Dr. Munch, the arts enhance basic skill learning. In fact, the arts are basic."

He said, "Your test results had better demonstrate that." And he comes in to our room at least once a week and sits in the back of the class taking notes. Mrs. Trilling just goes on about her business.

"First, I would like to tell you a story. Listen carefully. It's all about a beast called the polegar. The monster wasn't a polar bear or a tiger or even an alligator, but it had aspects of all three." Then she gave a loud grunt and started leaping around the room with her arms and hands all tangled up like crossed wires. She can be very dramatic.

"The polegar slept all winter in a cave on top of a mountain, but when spring came, he would wake up with a loud burp and careen down the cliff eating everything in sight. The people in the village could tell he was coming by the whiff of his grunt, a combination of sauerkraut and spoiled fruit."

We all went "Yuck!"

"His long body began to expand like a balloon from all the small animals, plants, and people he stuffed in his mouth with his spiky claws. His scaly body kept him from slipping on the steep hill. The villagers screamed and tried to escape, but most of the time he would eat his fill, gnash his pointy teeth with satisfaction, roll his one enormous bloodshot eye, and crawl back up to his cave until the next spring." She paused. "How do you think the story should end?"

A few of us raised our hands. She called on Rachel.

"A little girl who is hiding behind a tree pricks him with a big needle; he explodes, allowing all the people whom he swallowed whole to get away." Rachel glanced over at Mindy and I knew what she was thinking. She would have liked to stick a pin in Mindy. She was fuming at me, too. I felt like a rubber ball bouncing back and forth between them, but I didn't want to land on either side.

36

"The remains of the polegar disintegrate," concluded Rachel, "and that's that."

"Excellent," said Mrs. Trilling. "Now, can you all picture the polegar in your mind from my description?" Everyone nodded. "You can smell, see, and hear it?" We nodded again. "Good. Now each group has a bag containing identical materials. I'm going to give you the opportunity to construct your very own polegar. There are just a couple of rules." We can always count on Mrs. Trilling to have a few rules. "Each group must make the polegar without any talking whatsoever; yet the whole group has to agree about each feature of the polegar. Also, since you are trying to make an interesting, well-made polegar, be careful to put it together as carefully as possible. You have twenty minutes."

Everyone began ripping the bags open; they contained newspaper, scissors, Scotch tape, colored paper, and pipe cleaners. No one said a word. Just at that moment, Dr. Munch duck-walked in. He sat down with a bewildered sigh. Mrs. Trilling acknowledged him with a cheery wave.

Mindy, Rachel, Carolyn, and I were in a group. Every time Rachel would start to add a piece to the polegar, Mindy would shake her head and push her hand away. I wanted to push Mindy's hand away once when she stuck a stupid piece of blue paper in the middle, but I didn't dare. I wouldn't like one of Mindy's outbursts directed at me. She can be brutal when someone disagrees with her. Then she makes it seem like the other person's fault. This time I didn't want her taking over, but I didn't know how to stop her. Hoping my chance would come, I began to watch what was going on in the group. Whatever Carolyn or I added to the polegar, Mindy approved; she continued disregarding Rachel, who finally stopped participating.

We stuffed the bag with newspaper for the body, cut out a huge eye from the red-colored paper, and made long, pointy feet with the pipe cleaners. The group next to us had put their bag over Neil's head and were making him into a polegar. Everyone was having a great time except Dr. Munch and Rachel, who finally just sat back in her chair and started drawing with her Magic Marker. Our polegar didn't look very scary. It looked more like a chubby little dwarf with one eye.

"Time's up," said Mrs. Trilling. "How did it feel to make your polegar without talking? Tracy?" Tracy didn't answer. She just giggled.

Lonnie Nuell said, "At first we had a hard time trying to figure out how to communicate, but then we all started working together. I think if we had talked, we might have taken a lot longer to come to any decisions."

"Were there any leaders in your groups, or did everyone have an equal chance to use their ideas?" Mrs. Trilling asked.

The other six groups said they all worked equally. Carolyn, Mindy, and I avoided answering. Rachel had her arms folded and her eyes on the ceiling. Mrs. Trilling noticed, but she didn't say anything. "Now, I would like you all to examine each other's work so we can talk about the effectiveness of each polegar. Do they look the way I described a polegar in the story? Can they be considered pieces of sculpture? As a matter of fact, the Chicago Art

Institute is having a polegar exhibit and they want us to decide which polegar should be entered from our class." Everyone laughed but Dr. Munch. "You see, boys and girls, this project not only helps you discover your ability to work together in groups," her eyes rested on Mindy, "but also," she continued, "this aids in building a common vocabulary about works of art."

Jill would have said, " 'There's always a method to Mrs. Trilling's madness.' Shakespeare," because she was taking us to a sculpture exhibit next week.

I looked at our polegar and jotted down, "Can things that are ugly be beautiful, too, because of the way they're made or how they make us feel?" I looked around at the other polegars. Ours was having trouble staying up. It kept toppling over on its eye. I wrote another observation in small print so no one could see: "If our group had worked better together, maybe our polegar would have, too. We didn't have as much fun as the other groups, either."

Neil, who was still being a polegar, thumped over to me. His fingernails were covered with long, pointy pieces of colored paper, which he dangled menacingly in my face. "Will you be my polegarette?" he croaked. Even Dr. Munch smiled at that one. The best polegar had a gaping leer pasted on a shaggy newspaper face. There wasn't even any Scotch tape visible. I decided that as polegars go, it worked, and now I knew why. I could compare it with the rest of the other polegars.

Dr. Munch slipped out of the room after he told Mrs. Trilling to stop in his office later. We spent the next hour making a list of descriptive words about polegars and discussing how we might have built them differently. Neil suggested that we do a play with him as the lead polegar. We decided to construct a giant one for the entrance of the school. "Only we'll call it Dr. Munch," said Mindy.

At lunch, Mindy pushed two tables together so all the girls could surround her. Rachel ate alone, even after I asked her to join. She was being stubborn again. I didn't blame her exactly, but I couldn't help wishing she wasn't so thin-skinned.

When the dismissal bell rang, Mindy told me to come over. I said I had to go home and observe my fish. "Are you really doing that?" she said. "I'll just make up my report at the last minute. Murgatroyd never does anything different anyway."

Mother had scribbled another entry in her notebook.

> I find myself losing interest in these fish, but here I sit hour after hour—watching, waiting for something to happen. Sometimes I find myself losing track of time and space when I see the fish swirling round and round in the tank, sliding in and out of the leaves, coming up to kiss the surface, diving down, wiggling their tails gracefully. I become enveloped in the swirling color and the soft, flowing greenery.

I wrote a note to Mother: "This is a research project, not a creative-writing assignment." Clearly she needed help. In fact, I could tell from her writing that "The Fish Tale" was beginning to drive her berserk. The challenge was to establish some sort of contact with the fish. My plan was as follows: Every evening at their feeding time, I would put the top of my finger in the bowl. As soon as the flakes are sprinkled in, the fish swim to the surface and pucker up for their dinner. Goggles always lags behind, Shabunkin darts right up, and Goldy, the dainty queen, manages to get her fair share with a royal swish of her tail. I was hoping that the fish would begin nibbling at my finger, and eventually, they might be conditioned to nip my finger without their food. I would explain the plan to Mother when she came home.

She marched right in, slamming the back door. "Congratulate me," she said. "I unstuck the door myself. Took me all morning."

"It was about time." Then I told her about my brilliant idea.

But contrary to my expectations, she wasn't overly thrilled. "According to my professor," she said, "you're not following the traditional notions about a naturalistic study."

"What do you mean?" I asked, puzzled.

"The researcher isn't supposed to interfere with the subjects. The fish should be observed without any outside influence on our part that might change their behavior."

"But that depends on how you view your investigation," interjected Jill. "According to Willems and Raush, 1969, if a high degree of influence on the part of the researcher can be defended, Anabeth's methods are perfectly all right."

"What's your defense?" asked Mother. "I'm willing to try anything. These goldfish are driving me crazy."

"Well," I said, "I'm establishing a new way for fish enthusiasts to enjoy their fish." I didn't mention Mrs. Rumplemeyer's warning.

"It could be a major breakthrough," said Jill, "and the

fact that Anabeth is a participant observer in the events of the phenomena being studied does not make her less objective." Jill always sounds so smart.

"True," said Mother. "Her ego is not involved. She's just setting up a situation and watching to see what happens."

So it was settled. The Great Fish-Tale Experiment began.

5 ~ "Is it easier to be hated than ignored?"

For the next week, every time I sprinkled Tasty Tidbits in, I put the tip of my finger in the bowl. The first day, Goldy nipped at me curiously and then darted down to the bottom, followed by the other two. Instead of eating their food at the surface, all three waited until the flakes filtered down. The next night I tried again. The fish fluttered around in a great state of agitation. Maybe Mrs. Rumplemeyer was right. Maybe I was making them nervous. The third night, I dipped my finger in once more. Somehow, as if they were on guard, the goldfish waited for the food to drop down. By the end of the week, all three began swimming to the top again for their food, but avoided my finger. Frustrated, I wrote in my journal: "Maybe everyone's right. Except for porpoises and man-eating sharks, fish don't respond to people. I'm about to give up."

When Jill read my journal entry, she said, "It's easier to be hated than ignored."

"Who said that?"

"Some fading beauty" was her reply.

"Well, my report is due soon and nothing's happening."

"Maybe you've just invented a useless situation like raking up scattered leaves to build a fire."

Mother kept hoping that the fish would acknowledge me, too. "After all," she said, "my research paper depends on you, and so far we have zilch."

Her last entry said, "I have established a happy, healthy home for the fish, but aside from eating, sleeping, and brushing up against each other like cats, they aren't doing anything unusual."

Maybe nothing was going on with the goldfish, but at school plenty was happening. The rumor was that Dr. Munch had told Mrs. Trilling, "If you don't stop doing all those art projects and start teaching reading and math, you might not be around next year." Mindy heard the teachers dishing that dirt along with the baked beans at lunch. "But," said Mindy, "Mrs. Trilling made a bet with Dr. Munch that she could raise our reading scores using her own methods." I thought about my own experiment and wished Mrs. Trilling good luck to myself. Our class has about as much ability as those silly goldfish. Me included. Mindy has me laughing so much all day long with her antics that it's hard to pay attention. When I try and tell her I need to work, she keeps needling me. Fortunately, I've already completed most of the sections in math and reading. I don't know what I would have done if Mindy had turned up at the beginning of the year. She's a welcome change of pace, but at the same time, I feel guilty goofing off.

The only one who's not laughing at Mindy is Rachel, who's become a real spoilsport. She never wants to be with the rest of us any more and is always giving me dirty looks.

"It's almost the end of the school year, so we might as well have some fun," I told her.

"You call this fun?" Rachel said the day Mindy set off the fire alarm and we had to evacuate the whole building. We stood outside in the rain for an hour before they let us back in. Rachel had a point there. But she wouldn't help with *The Skokie Scuttlebutt,* either. Neither would Mindy, who decided we should spend our free periods playing kickball or messing around instead. I didn't disagree. Let someone else be the big organizer for a change. The newspaper wouldn't work without Rachel anyway.

Mindy thinks Rachel's jealous just because we're friends. "She's just a goody-goody," said Mindy to me at lunch one day. "She's trying to impress the teachers."

"Let's face it. Rachel wants to get good grades. You're so far behind in your math workbook, you may never catch up. Rachel's already past sixth-grade level," I said in a joking voice. But I was serious. Mindy never did her work.

"Don't worry," said Mindy with a sly wink. "I took Rachel's last three work sheets when she put them on Mrs. Trilling's desk. I've already copied the answers and stuck them back in her folder."

"You what?" I almost shrieked. "That's cheating.

You'll never get away with it." This was one time that I almost wished she wouldn't. Those work sheets had taken me hours to do.

"Wanna bet?" said Mindy.

"If Rachel finds out, she'll tell."

"She better not if she knows what's good for her."

Right after lunch, Mrs. Trilling told Mindy to come down to Dr. Munch's office with her. Carolyn whispered to me, "Do you think she's in trouble?"

Tracy said, "If she is, Mindy will know how to get out of it."

I looked over at Rachel as if to say, "You're in hot water now." She jerked open her desk and blocked my view. Rachel is just as tough as Mindy in her own way. I didn't know what I would do in the same situation. All I knew was that Mindy would retaliate and the rest of the class would back her up. It's an unwritten law that we don't report each other. Even when Neil poured red paint all over Carolyn's new sneakers, she didn't turn him in.

When Mindy and Mrs. Trilling came back, Mindy looked as if she'd been crying and Mrs. Trilling gave us a long speech about honesty being the best policy, and that once we start lying, we might develop the habit. I've never seen her so upset. She went on and on until I finally stopped listening and began staring at a poster of a bird sitting on the top of Ziggy's head, which read, "Stay on the straight and narrow and you'll never have to worry about bumping into anyone."

"Why'd you have to go and tell Mrs. Trilling?" I demanded, confronting Rachel on the steps after school.

"Tell her what?" Rachel's jaw was set and I knew she wouldn't budge an inch.

"How else could Mrs. Trilling know that Mindy took your papers?"

"It wouldn't take a genius to figure out that Mindy copied from me. How else could such a dummy get all the answers right?"

"You didn't have to go tattling on her," I said, not convinced one way or the other. "Why make a big fuss over work sheets?"

"But I never said she could use them. She thinks she can do whatever she wants and get away with it."

"But telling the teacher," I said, "that's being a fink."

"Whether I told or not isn't the point," Rachel said fiercely. "She cheated and that's not fair. You're going to stick up for her anyway, so why bother discussing this?"

"Look," I almost shouted into her stubborn face, "you haven't been so nice to me lately, either. You scuttled *The Skokie Scuttlebutt* and you sit around scribbling all the time." Rachel stared at me with such a hard look that I wanted to shove her, slam, right through the wall she had built between us and knock it down. "Why did you have to make such a big fuss about those stupid work sheets?"

"It's not just the work sheets and you know it. Anyway, I'd rather be drawing anytime than following Mindy Gottfried around the way you are."

"I'm not following her around. You don't care about your friends—especially me," I yelled.

"Just forget it," Rachel said.

Why was the world always black or white for her? Why was I stuck in this predicament? I turned away.

Rachel shouldn't have told on Mindy. And I wasn't following after her.

Everyone gathered around Mindy. "What happened? What did they do to you?" we all wanted to know.

"Let's go back to my house," said Mindy. "There are certain people around here with big ears and big mouths."

Rachel walked by us without even turning her head.

We sat around Mindy's glass-top dining-room table. I could see Carolyn's toes curling nervously in her sandals. Mindy had her hands clenched together in a fist, and I felt as if my knees were locked. Everyone looked so intent that I was reminded of a group of generals meeting to discuss a battle.

"This is war," said Mindy. "That little brat Rachel told the teacher I stole her papers, and all I did was borrow them to check my answers." She looked at me quickly. I kept my mouth shut, but I was beginning to get a lumpy feeling in my chest. Was I the only one who knew she was lying?

"That's the worst thing I've ever heard," said Tracy. "Was Dr. Munch mean to you? Is he going to call your mother?"

"They made a big deal out of it," said Mindy scornfully. "Natasha's going to be furious." I could picture Natasha, red nails poised like arrows over Mindy's head.

"Rachel's stuck up," said Tracy, "just because she thinks she's so smart."

"Rachel's not stuck up," I wanted to say, "she's just shy." But Rachel had been snubbing me lately, too. In fact, Rachel had been acting impossible. Our last conversation proved that even I couldn't talk to her any more.

Mindy said, "Well, Miss Toadeyes is going to be sorry."

"What should we do?" asked Carolyn. She looked excited about the whole thing. So did Tracy.

"We'll have to leave a hate note in her desk every day," said Mindy. "We used to do that in Highland Park when someone was obnoxious."

"You write them, Carolyn," she continued. "You're so clever." Carolyn beamed. "And no one say a word to her at school. If she asks a question, just turn your head away."

"We can corner her on the playground," said Tracy. "I think you should tell her off, Mindy."

So far, I hadn't said a word. Three against one. I almost wanted to call Rachel and tell her not to come to school—to pretend she had mononucleosis or measles or something. But Rachel would probably ignore me. She didn't care what I said, anyway.

"Everyone can make up a list this weekend," said Mindy, "and we can meet again Monday after school." Carolyn and Tracy nodded. I could just imagine what they would come up with. I felt queasy and uncomfortable. I wanted to go home, but was afraid of what I would miss, of what they might say if I left.

Lorna strutted in the room. She was wearing tight jeans and three-inch wooden heels. "I can tell you little twerps are up to something," she said. "You look like the cats that swallowed the canary."

"Just get out of here," said Mindy.

"I know your sister, Jill," said Lorna, curling her lip at me like Mindy does. "She's a real brain, isn't she?"

"I guess so," I mumbled.

"Well, she's always in the library with her friends. I think they're a bunch of snobs." No wonder Mindy acts tough, with a sister like Lorna.

The doorbell rang. It was Natasha. "I forgot my damn key again," she said crossly. "Come on in, Seymour," she said to a big, burly man with a fuzzy gray beard. The Gottfrieds' household was getting more like a soap opera every day.

Poking his head through the door, Seymour said, "Hey, folks, what's happening?" They were wearing matching black T-shirts which said MARCH 3 in bright-pink, sequinned letters. They were holding hands. Seymour looked about fifty years older than Natasha. I wondered if he was going to be the rich next husband. Lorna gave him a smile of sticks, her lips set in a thin, straight line, and went into her bedroom.

"What's the date stand for?" asked Carolyn.

"That was the night of our first date," explained Natasha. "Seymour manufactures shirts." His arm oozed over her shoulder like a jellyfish. "Mindy," Natasha snapped, "you better do all the dishes and sweep up the kitchen."

"Why do I have to? It's Lorna's turn," Mindy whined.

"Now!" she screamed. "Or else!" She and Seymour disappeared into the bedroom.

"I've gotta go now," I said. This time, all the snarling and yelling at the Gottfrieds' were too much for me. "I have to go take care of my goldfish," I announced, standing up.

"Call me later," commanded Mindy.

6 ⊱ "People in glass houses shouldn't throw stones"

Monday morning, Mrs. Trilling gathered us together for our expedition to the Art Institute. "Choose your bus partner and line up by twos at the door." Out of habit I looked around for Rachel. We've been bus partners since first grade. Mindy grabbed my hand. Everyone went scrambling across the room to find someone. Rachel ended up alone at the back of the line. Carolyn and Tracy were poking each other, pretending to tell secrets about her. "*Rrribbet. Rrribbet*," they croaked.

Mrs. Trilling called out, "Come up to the front, Rachel. You can be my partner." Mindy gave out a loud guffaw as Rachel walked by us. "Stick out your foot next time," she ordered me.

The bus ride was cramped and stuffy even with the windows open. Right away we all started singing. Mindy led the girls in a rousing version of "I've Been Workin' on the Railroad." Then the boys drowned us out with "A Hundred Bottles of Beer on the Wall." We were screaming at the top of our lungs until the bus driver outmaneuvered us by pulling over to the side of Interstate 70 and yelling, "Shut up or this bus stays here!"

My father used to do that on family trips. Jill would tell him, "A woman convinced against her will is not convinced."

The art museum is a huge limestone building with at least thirty steps to climb. On either side of the door are enormous bronze lions. I was feeling hot and tired. I hoped one of those museum ladies in the pink pinafores wouldn't be waiting there to lead us around. They instruct us to listen quietly to a long, boring spiel about who did what when, to walk in a line, and please not to touch the art objects. "Keep your grubby claws off the paintings," yelled Neil as we tramped in.

Two museum guards in blue uniforms met us at the entrance. Mrs. Trilling handed them a piece of paper. One of them gave it a cursory glance and motioned us into the great hall, which has a high, dome-shaped ceiling. No lady in a pink apron was anywhere in sight.

Mrs. Trilling said, "Spread yourselves out and let's loosen up. Shake out your arms and legs, and jump up and down."

Wiggling her face and wrinkling her nose, she stretched her mouth into a wide O. *Ooooooo ouuuuuuu eeeeeeee* were the sounds that emerged. We all followed suit. "Something different is about to happen," I told Mindy. She wasn't participating, but Mrs. Trilling never forces anyone to do anything.

"What's with these crazy exercises?" asked Mindy crossly.

"Mrs. Trilling just has unusual ideas. When you've been here longer, you'll get used to doing odd things in odd places," I said. But Mindy wasn't listening. She was mouthing a loud *Ooooooooooo*, right in Rachel's ear. Rachel moved away from her and closer to Mrs. Trilling. "Teacher's pet," spat Carolyn.

"Now face your neighbor," called Mrs. Trilling. I found myself staring into Rachel's soft brown eyes. I couldn't tell what she was thinking.

"One of you become a mirror with the other person looking into the mirror. Now all of you mirrors watch very closely what your partner is doing and copy their actions." I decided to be the mirror. Rachel began bending and swaying, her arms swinging up and down.

"Use your eyes; be observant; get into what the other person is doing," instructed Mrs. Trilling. Rachel and I didn't say anything to each other, but soon we were moving simultaneously. I could almost tell what she was going to do before she even initiated the action. Our arms formed large arcs, then small ones. We swooped and looped in time to a rhythm that our bodies were forming.

"Very nice," called Mrs. Trilling. "You all look like sculptures that have come to life." Then we were following her out of the great hall, through the arched doors, and down a narrow corridor. I was much more relaxed now. Mindy came up behind me. "I saw you with Miss Toadeyes," she said. "Did you tell her off?"

"No, I just sort of ignored her," I answered. For a while it had been like old times with Rachel. I almost forgot that we were mad at each other, even though we hadn't spoken since the work-sheet incident. But I couldn't bring myself to tell that to Mindy.

Mrs. Trilling led us into a new wing of the museum. The room was white, with a skylight that flooded the space with sunshine. On the walls were enormous, brightly colored paintings. "Let's gather in a big circle," she said. "I'm going to call out some colors, and as I do, think about how that color makes you feel. You don't need to say anything, but show me with your bodies what you are experiencing." Rapidly she named red, green, blue; then yellow, black, and pink. With red I had a throbbing, pulsating impression. Blue was calm and peaceful; yellow bright and cheerful; black gave me a gloomy, dark sensation, like being shut in. My eyes were closed but I moved my body as she named each color. Then I saw all the colors flickering on and off in my mind, blending and changing like a kaleidoscope. The glints of color reminded me of my goldfish glimmering in the water as they swam round and round.

Mrs. Trilling told us to look at a large, vertical stripe painting. It must have been twenty-five feet long. There were ten rows of colors. "Find the color that attracts you and stand in front of it." I chose red. "Focus very hard on your color." I let the red surround me like a cloak. I like the excitement of the color red.

Mindy chose purple. "Like a queen," she said.

Rachel stood in front of the black. "Black is for a witch," said Tracy.

Neil knocked against me. "I figured you would choose red," he said.

"Why?"

"Cause red is for show-offs."

"That's you, not me," I said.

"Then we make a good pair."

I scooted over to yellow.

"All right," Mrs. Trilling announced, "lie down on the floor on your backs and continue to concentrate on your stripe colors."

"Oh, God," moaned Mindy. "Now she wants us to get down on the floor. This is getting ridiculous."

I stretched out between Neil and Mindy. Neil stuck his leg over mine. I pushed it off. "Sex fiend," I told him.

"Notice how your color looks between its neighbors. Does it change or move? Watch three or four stripes at a time." I noticed that the red began to look dark next to the blue and green. Then it started to vibrate and become brighter. At first the painting looked like a flat design of stripes, and now it was as if each column was pushing and pulling out from the wall.

"Stand up now; look at the entire painting and then we'll move on," said Mrs. Trilling.

The next room took me completely by surprise. A rambling structure composed of large plates of smoky, transparent glass filled the space. The walls of the sculpture zigzagged around, reminding me of a maze or the tilted fun house at a carnival.

"This is a walk-through sculpture by a California artist named Larry Bell, called 'The Iceberg and Its Shadow,' " explained Mrs. Trilling. Then I realized that the piece was divided into two sections. A smaller glass house of darker gray hovered like a shadow next to the larger one. The triangular and rectangular shapes were joined together, but I could see through all sides, to all corners, in every direction.

"How can she call this sculpture?" scoffed Mindy. "It looks like somebody stuck a lot of glass plates together and propped them up."

Mrs. Trilling plugged in a tape recorder and turned on some music. It was soft . . . rippling harp and piano. "Walk through 'The Iceberg and Its Shadow,'" she said. "Take your time. Explore it, search for the hidden. Try not to talk, but interact with each other. Afterward, we can sit down and share our impressions."

Soon we were all moving through the sculpture, peering at our reflections and at each other through the glass, which turned from brownish-yellow, blue, purple, smoky gray to blue again. Reflections collided; faces were transformed. I thought of frost on windowpanes, a misty mountaintop, a low-lying cloud, then a cave. I wanted to touch the sleek, beveled edges.

Mindy pranced by. "I am the ice queen in my ice castle," she sang. She motioned to me. I wanted to go the other way, but I followed her instead.

Carolyn sailed by. "I've counted fifty-six sheets of glass," she proclaimed. Carolyn, the counter, namer of names, was always one for facts and figures.

I wanted to escape into the cool, strange world of the iceberg again. The tape changed to electronic music. Sharp, discordant sounds echoed through the glass corridors. Mindy disappeared abruptly round a corner. I gazed through the glass. Rachel was on the other side making sharp movements to the music. Her face was blurred. I pressed my face up against the smooth, clear wall. We started bending and reaching in time to the music as we had in the mirror game. I was a puppet making funny faces. Who was pulling the strings? I seemed to be walking inside a mirror—losing myself in mirrors of time and space—sharing. The sculpture, Rachel, and I were one.

The tape changed again to the music from *Star Wars*. The mood was broken. I continued on my way. Neil and Billy were pretending to be Martian robots, their legs and arms extended stiffly. Strange beeps came from their mouths. Then the music stopped and Mrs. Trilling called us to come out. I hoped we wouldn't have to sit down and talk about the experience right away. I needed to mull it over in my head first.

"The bus has to leave now if we want to return to school before lunch," Mrs. Trilling said. "Perhaps when you go home you might jot down some of your thoughts about today's adventure." I was already making up a poem in my head about mirrors, shadows, and puppets without strings.

As I climbed on the bus with Mindy, I noticed that Rachel was sitting alone. She was sketching the iceberg in quick, easy strokes. I paused to look at her drawing. At the bottom she had written, "People in glass houses shouldn't throw stones." I wanted to sit down beside her, but a little voice inside me said, "*No!* Keep on going," and I realized I was afraid.

7 ❧ "With friends like you, who needs enemies?"

Mrs. Trilling hung Rachel's drawing on the bulletin board, but it didn't help, because for the next few weeks Mindy, Carolyn, and Tracy made Rachel's life miserable. One afternoon, they backed her up into the fence on the playground, called her Toadeyes, and made her say please to get by. And Rachel did say please twice. First she used a high-and-mighty voice, but when they wouldn't move, she sounded so plaintive and whimpery that everyone started mimicking her. They put signs in her desk that said DANGER! TOUCH TOADEYES AND YOU'LL GET WARTS!

"Kiss the frog, Neil," said Mindy, "and you'll turn into a toad." Rachel hung back, taking all their guff, even when they blocked her way to the bathroom. She said, "Please, please," in such a resigned, simpering way that I was embarrassed for her. No one would sit next to her at lunch after that.

"Let's face it," declared Mindy, "she's poison and she

knows it." The one thing Mindy didn't do was take her homework again.

Maybe Mrs. Trilling hoped Rachel could work the problem out herself; maybe she didn't notice what was going on, because she never said anything. Rachel never said anything, either, but she was eager as ever to please the teacher. Her hand would shoot up in the air every time Mrs. Trilling asked a question. She walked around with a forlorn face, but not once did she try and defend herself. I figured that if she wanted to be an outcast that was her problem, but I wasn't about to pick on her the way Mindy and the others did. Occasionally, I gave her a piercing glance, as if to say, "Don't just sit there, do something!" But Rachel's attitude seemed to be "Don't do anything, just sit there."

And Mindy had taken over the class. She knew what everyone was doing all the time. She called me three times a night. She checked up on Carolyn and Tracy, too. At school she kept busy passing notes and whispering. All the girls did what she said now. Every once in a while I would tell her to stop being so bossy, but she wouldn't listen. She was so outrageous she could even outsmart the teachers. By sheer cockiness, she made people pay attention to her whether they liked her or not.

One morning, as Mother and I were hovering over the fish, she said, "Where has Rachel been? I haven't seen her around here or heard you talking about her for several weeks."

"She's been sick," I said.

Mother gave me a "that's a likely story" look.

"Rachel's mother called me yesterday." I looked down as if the linoleum pattern on the floor fascinated me. "She wondered if you had said anything to me about Rachel. Rachel doesn't want to go to school any more. She just wants to stay home with her oil paints. Mrs. Horwitz is thinking of going to the school and talking with the guidance counselor if this continues."

I was mute as a turnip.

Jill, who was lounging in the hammock outside the door, called out, "I'll bet that Mindy Gottfried is giving her trouble. She's the kind of friend that knifes you in the front instead of the back." Jill's friends are all studious and square like Rachel. She doesn't know what it's like to have a friend like Mindy. She might be a troublemaker, but she's not dull.

Mother looked at me very intently. Advice was forthcoming. I prepared to make a quick getaway. "I'm not one of those mothers who likes to butt into their children's affairs . . ."

Here it comes, I thought, the big BUT!

". . . but Rachel has always been your good friend. If she's having any problems, she might need a buddy to support her."

"She's got her nose stuck in the air lately," I said. "Anyway, I can't."

"Why not?"

"I just can't."

My family would never understand. They think Rachel is so sweet. They don't know how moody and stubborn she can be. And just because Mindy isn't Jill's type, Jill bugs me about her.

"With friends like you, who needs enemies?" Jill couldn't resist making a remark.

"Who asked for your opinion?" I screamed, and headed off in the direction of the den, a good place to hide when I'm in a rotten mood. Jill made me sick with all her stupid quotations. As I pulled open the heavy oak door, I heard Mother call out a loud "Whoops!" followed by "You little rascal!" I knew she wasn't talking to me, so I ran back to the kitchen. There was Shabunkin leaping right out of the water, landing with a startled splash, and throwing himself up again.

"He's going to fall out on the counter and kill himself," I screeched, horrified, and at the same time glad the pressure was off me.

"Phone the police; telegram Mrs. Rumplemeyer; call in the rescue squad. Gawd! All this hullabaloo over a crazy fish," groaned Jill.

"Calm down, old high flier," I coaxed . . . Another contorted, disrespectful leap.

"We'll have to get a wire screen and attach it over the top of the bowl," said Mother.

"But if we do that," I cried, "I can't stick my finger in and that will ruin my experiment."

"Well, we can't take the chance of the fish flipping out of there again."

"There must be another solution," I moaned.

"Why don't you just remove some of the water. It's obvious that the bowl is filled with too much water," said Jill.

Jill and her IQ came in handy occasionally. I had to admit her suggestion had merit.

So the experiment continued. Shabunkin gave up, and that night at feeding time Goggles swam to the top and nipped my finger. I cheered and spent the next hour scribbling in my journal. A major breakthrough!

4/28. Today Goggles swam around my finger and then nipped me several times. I was careful not to move. The other fish ignored me as usual. He then went about the business of having his dinner and swam back down among the leaves.

4/29. Goggles was the first up for dinner tonight. He nipped at my finger again, swished his tail, and then swam away. My friends at school don't believe my story, but I'm sure he's aware of me now.

For the next week, each time I put the food and my finger in the bowl, the black fish would greet me. The others continued to avoid my finger. I was enjoying myself now.

"Why don't you try another time of day," suggested my father. "I think the fish thinks you're a big flake."

"Cynic!" I laughed.

At school, Mindy, Tracy, and Carolyn continued giving Rachel the cold treatment, but they were too busy planning a party for Mindy's birthday to play any more pranks on her.

Rachel looked less distant, and at lunch she started sitting with Lonnie Nuell, a girl I didn't know very well, who had moved here from California in September.

8 ❧ "Cross that bridge when you come to it"

It was a rainy May afternoon as the four of us slogged our way through the muddy field to Mindy's block. More than a heavy drizzle, the rain had started early and continued all day. The cold gray stone apartments of Davenport Drive loomed up solidly in the distance. My sneakers were already hopeless, so I sloshed around in the deep puddles. I was hanging on the edge of the group—excited jabberers planning a celebration. My shoes made gurgling splats. I paid more attention to that weird sound than to Carolyn, Tracy, and Mindy. Maybe it was the gloomy day and the fact that I had forgotten my plastic parka so my clothes were drenched, but I didn't feel like joining in the discussion. Some days I just wanted to be with one person, and Mindy always traveled in groups.

"It's a good thing we're having dinner at my house tonight so we can make arrangements," Mindy was saying. She turned around to look at me, the one stray from the pack. "Keep up with us," she teased. "Slowpoke." Oh, she could be bossy all right, but then she was tugging my hand, prancing around me, wheedling me back with her funny remarks and silly dance. She never stopped running the show. Through sheer force of energy, Mindy could outdo and undo me. She would eventually inveigle me to become enthusiastic about her party. She always did, so I shed my invisible loner's cape and moved in step with the Fabulous Foursome—Mindy's new name for us. It established our solidarity, our specialness.

"What I like about parties with a theme," Mindy said as we climbed her wooden stairs, "is that they are a complete surprise to everyone. They're more fun. In Highland Park, Lorna had a Fifties Sock Hop last year. Dynamite! ! !"

This I wanted to hear more about, but clambering down the steps from the opposite direction were Natasha and Seymour, dressed in identical white tennis outfits. Two white flags soaring above us. The shirts said I'D RATHER BE SAILING. Good old Seymour!

"It's pouring down rain," remarked Mindy, eyeing Seymour suspiciously.

"We play indoors, ma'dear," he said, releasing a loud, honking laugh, making his beard curl up around his toothy grin. He was neither impressed nor puzzled by Mindy's rudeness. There were some worlds she couldn't rule.

Natasha shot Mindy a warning look and patted Seymour possessively on the arm. "Take off those soggy shoes at the door," she ordered, and a minute later we heard the low hum of Seymour's MG as they sped off.

Mindy looked in that direction with a vague look of contempt. I was secretly thankful that my parents weren't auditioning for new partners. A Seymour would be hard to take.

"Natasha has a closetful of new T-shirts," said Mindy. I didn't have to ask her what she thought of him.

"Well." Tracy tittered. "At least if you run out, you know who to ask." Mindy's sneer turned from vague to prominent. I stifled an impulse to laugh.

"Tell us about the Fifties Sock Hop," interjected Carolyn. After all, we had trooped over there for a purpose. Time to drop a sticky subject and get on with it.

Mindy's eyes widened with renewed interest and she began explaining that the invitations were important. Lorna had sent everyone a 45 record with details written on the label. She had decorated the house with posters of Elvis Presley, high-school pennants, pictures of hot rods, and plenty of balloons to pop. Everyone arrived with greased hair, ponytails, bobby socks, and pleated skirts. She served Hot Diggity Hot Dogs and Tutti-Frutti-o'-Rooty Punch.

"Sounds great," breathed Tracy. Sounds corny, I thought, but then Lorna sock-hopping around saying "Nifty" and "Shake, rattle, and roll" seemed unlikely. I could picture her as a dance-hall mama at a Wild West party, or as Dracula's Daughter on Halloween, but not as a rosy-cheeked doo-wah doo-wopping American bandstander.

Mindy, I could tell, wanted a party that would run rings around Lorna's Sock Hop, and it was our duty as members of the Fabulous Foursome to come up with a clever idea. Organizing was Mindy's strong point, not ideas.

Flipping through Lorna's party-ideas book, Carolyn suggested a Mystery Mixer with puzzles as invitations, a scavenger hunt, I Spy Pizza, and FBIce Treats. Tracy favored the Carnival Party with balloon invitations, game booths, crepe-paper streamers, and Grandstand ice-cream sandwiches. "We could have games like Eggs-tra Eggs-iting Egg Throw and signs decorating it like THE YOLK'S ON YOU or BE AN EGGS-PERT," I added, dutifully enthused.

Mindy wasn't convinced yet, so we discussed an Outer Space Odyssey with a Galaxy of Games; a Hooray for Hollywood Costume Party with Hollywood Hero Sandwiches, Starring Rolls, and Celebrity Sweetshakes; then a Roaring Twenties Party, a Jungle Jamboree, and a Hawaiian Luau.

Just as my stomach began to rumble from hunger, we settled on a Monster Bash with demonish decorations, ghoulish games, and fang-tastic food, which satisfied Mindy and promised to be more fun than a barrel of bats. I hoped Carl would show up and whip up another batch of his tacos before I collapsed from hunger. I needed to refuel before I could face making bat invitations out of black construction paper.

"When's the next full moon?" asked Tracy. "The party ought to be on that night."

"Let's have it at my house," I suggested.

"Your house is too fancy," said Mindy.

I gulped. My house was big, but fancy? No way. Just a lot of comfortable overstuffed chairs and couches, shelves filled with books, and cozy rooms to hide away in. Why did she have to say that?

"We have to plan the guest list, too," said Carolyn.

"I think we should invite everyone in the class," I said. Mindy dismissed that idea immediately, but I would press it later. Mother had always insisted that I invite the whole class to parties. She didn't like the idea of leaving anyone out.

No Carl, no Natasha, and no dinner. It was 7:30. My stomach sounded like a Mack truck. Carolyn and Tracy were fidgeting nervously, too. When Tim finally walked in at 8:00, I decided to pop the question.

"Are we having dinner here or what?" Mindy looked surprised, as if I were speaking Swahili.

"I've been waiting for Tim. He's going to drop us off at McDonald's." Three of the Fabulous Foursome broke into huge grins.

"I'll drop you off," he said, "but then you have to walk home."

Our faces fell, but Mindy didn't seem to notice. Carolyn, Tracy, and I looked at each other. McDonald's was in the middle of downtown Skokie and no place to walk home from at night. I wasn't even allowed to walk from a friend's house alone after dark.

"Let's go," said Mindy. "I'm ready for a Big Mac and French fries." Who could resist that? We piled into Tim's old Buick. I flashed back to another one of Mother's expressions at the thought of the impending hike home: "Cross that bridge when you come to it."

The bridge came sooner than I expected. Three chocolate milk shakes, three cheeseburgers, six orders of

French fries, and an apple pie later, we staggered out through the golden arches and prepared to hoof our way across the dark streets of Skokie.

I was rooted to the sidewalk as if I'd forgotten how to walk. I wasn't particularly alarmed about the danger, I just knew this was one of those rules I shouldn't be breaking. As a result, instead of refusing, I was simply incapable of movement. But Carolyn and Tracy began to complain about the long walk, the rain (which had ceased hours ago), the multitude of horrible criminals hiding behind every street lamp, and sudden stomach ailments. Mindy was incredulous, then amused by our protests. I envied her lack of concern, yet it occurred to me that Natasha didn't care one way or the other if she walked home. That thought enabled me to say, "Why don't I just call my mother? I know she'd be glad to come and get us." A positive suggestion. Relieved smiles on the faces of Carolyn and Tracy, a sullen look from Mindy. She didn't like not having her way. But I was tired of her telling us what to do, tired of tagging along. She was getting meaner and bossier every day. I was glad I'd spoken up, and relieved that Tracy and Carolyn agreed.

"Go ahead if you want to. Biggest bunch of babies I ever saw." She recovered several minutes later and shouted for us to climb up on the wall next to McDonald's to wait for Mother's Chevy wagon, but I could tell that she was irritated with me by the way she threw her arms around Carolyn's and Tracy's shoulders and left me standing on the corner.

Mother must have raced across Skokie in record time. She wondered why I hadn't called earlier, why I hadn't mentioned the McDonald's plan before, and what if she had been out? I changed the subject and told her about the Monster Bash. She reminded me to make sure everyone in the class was included, and Mindy, giving me another sullen glance, reluctantly agreed. I knew that I had won a small victory.

9 ❧ "The dinosaurs are not all dead"

Mindy handed out the invitations herself at school. Rachel looked surprised when she dumped one on her desk. Thirty black bats were unfurled with white cards that read "Right from the word ghoul, you're invited to a gory-ous, monster-ous bash. Here's your chance to be kooky and spooky."

Mrs. Trilling said, "This gives me a frightfully fun idea. The girls have made up a poem filled with double meanings. You find this kind of language being used all the time in what you say, what you read, and what you write." Then she wrote the word RIDDLES in big letters on the blackboard. She turned around with an air of expectancy and repeated the word "riddles" out loud.

"Here she goes again," Mindy said as she fidgeted at her desk. Mrs. Trilling had stolen her spotlight. "She'll probably have us flying around the room like bats any minute."

"I'd like you to listen to another poem," Mrs. Trilling continued. "Like the invitation, there is an extended way to interpret the words. Think of this poem as a riddle." Then she began reciting in her comic, theatrical voice:

A silver-scaled Dragon with jaws flaming red
Sits at my elbow and toasts my bread.
I hand him fat slices, and then, one by one,
He hands them back when he sees they are done.

Hands flew up all over the room. "It's about a dragon who is toasting some kid's bread," blurted Neil. More hands straining in the air.

"Do you think the poet may be talking about something more than a dragon?" Mrs. Trilling smiled, as if she and the poet were collaborators.

I said, "The dragon is a toaster. His flaming red jaws are really the electrical coils."

"Exactly," said Mrs. Trilling, enormously pleased at the nodding heads that greeted my pronouncement. "Does the poem give any other clues that the toaster reminds the poet of a dragon?" Rachel brought up the silver scales and the word "toast," which was certainly a big hint.

Then Mrs. Trilling read the poem by Carl Sandburg that begins "The fog comes on little cat feet," and I could picture the misty haze stealing silently into the city like a cat creeping over the rooftops at night. "Speaking of monsters," she said, "listen to this poem and see if you can figure it out."

The dinosaurs are not all dead.
I saw one raise its iron head
To watch me walking down the road

Beyond our house today.
Its jaws were dripping with a load
Of earth and grass that it had cropped.
It must have heard me where I stopped.
Snorted white steam my way,
And stretched its long neck out to see,
And chewed and grinned quite amiably.

Some people had trouble with that one. I realized immediately that the dinosaur was really a steam shovel. That's the way I usually see things, only I'm always comparing people to animals.

"Poets often view the world in metaphors," Mrs. Trilling was saying. "So do artists. Think about looking at the clouds. While you watch the shapes change, don't you think of all the strange objects they remind you of?" I was feeling a surge of excitement inside me. If artists and poets look at people and objects around them the same way I do, what does that make me? What I had always considered strange about myself might really be a gift. Just like Rachel's drawing. I looked over at her. I wished we could talk about this.

"Pet names or nicknames are a special kind of metaphoric language," said Mrs. Trilling. "And sometimes these names can be offensive and cause hurt feelings, like when you call someone who's fat a pig or someone who's shy a mouse. Words are full of images and it's fun to create different moods by playing around with figurative language. But I hope you won't use the power that words have to hurt someone else." Mindy stared back at her defiantly. Then we played a game of nicknames and everyone was very careful not to say "Toadeyes."

We played figurative language games straight through math, science, and social studies. Clearly our principal's warning to Mrs. Trilling that she should stick to the standard workbooks had gone in one ear and out the other. Mrs. Trilling's genius for thinking up creative schemes seemed to be spurred on by a little conflict. "I'm convinced," she told us, "that drill, rote, and memorizing are outmoded, no longer useful in the classroom." More likely than not, she was just as bored by testing and measuring as we were and thought up all these games to keep herself amused as well as a group of thirty sixth-graders. I noticed that other teachers at school looked at her in a peculiar manner, especially when she was seen coming in and out of the principal's office on more occasions than were normal during the regular school week. I guessed that she and Dr. Munch had some kind of deal going whereby she would prove that whatever it was that she was doing in the classroom was somehow working. I, for one, loved Mrs. Trilling. I appreciated her melodious voice rising and falling to make a story more graphic, or her large, bony frame lunging across the room to reinforce a point. I was writing poems in my head all the time now, and sometimes I even put them down on paper. I think Mrs. Trilling inspired me. Besides, making up poems was a way of pushing out of my mind all the intrigues going on at school. When Mindy's demands and scheming were too much for me, I would start doodling with words the way Rachel doodles with lines, and then let my imaginings take flight. Schoolwork was becoming interesting again.

I no longer made only strange, unusual comparisons.

My nose, eyes, and ears were suddenly alert to everything. I saw sunlight shimmering off the black metal of a fireplug. I saw shadows casting long, lean shapes on the sidewalk. I noiced an obese, jolly old man talking rapidly to himself at the bus stop. I heard the shattering of glass mingled with the shrill laughter of two boys running ahead of me through an alley. The aroma of fresh tar mingled with the smell of gasoline on the streets. How many times had I seen these same sights before? How many times? Now I was playing the images over and over in my mind and making up stories about them. Something new was happening to my senses.

If I felt myself plodding mindlessly around, I would hear Mrs. Trilling, her words reverberating down through tree trunks, from behind mailboxes, trash cans, and up from the gutters: Be curious. Look for beauty wherever you go. I tried to explain this new feeling to Mindy one afternoon on the way to her apartment to make decorations for the Monster Bash.

"Look at those two ladies gabbing on the bench." I pointed out their wide-brimmed hats, prim black suits, and white gloves. "Don't you wonder why they're so dressed up?"

"Those two old bags over there?" said Mindy without a trace of interest. "I didn't even notice them."

"I'll bet they don't have anywhere to go. They just sit there all day pretending they're about to go out to lunch or to a tea." I noticed their blue-gray hair was identical.

"What are you talking about?" asked Mindy. "What do you care?"

"I'm just curious, that's all," I said, hurt that she couldn't share in my speculations. I was already inventing a sad tale about them. I bent down to watch a spider that was spinning his web in the gutter. " 'The Black Widows.' That's what I'll call the story." But Mindy was already shouting orders down the street to the gang on the corner. She wanted to play kickball. I wanted to watch the spider some more. Once, in second grade, Rachel and I made up a play about spiders. She did the scenery; I wrote the script. Rachel created an elaborate web out of string that we set up in her basement. She painted flowers and grass on an old sheet, which she draped on the wall. My job was inventing silly little ditties for the spiders to say to each other. We invited our parents to watch. I wrote parts for them, too. My father said we were better than Broadway. I wondered if Rachel remembered.

Someone was breathing heavily at my side. I looked up. Mindy was eyeing me impatiently. "I've been yelling at you for five minutes. I need you on my team." She heaved the ball to me. "Now run and then throw it over." Automatically, I caught the ball and sprinted alongside her. No time to linger in the gutter. Mindy's games demanded full attention.

"Now toss it," she ordered as we headed down the street to join the game. "No, not that way! Can't you aim?" she screamed. I scrambled over to retrieve the ball, which was sliding into the bushes. I had to crawl under a thorny branch to find it. She made me so nervous I couldn't even catch a ball any more. What was I doing here? Why couldn't I just say I was tired of kickball and wanted to go home? But then I found myself joining the game and dashing around the field until I was all hot and sweaty.

"I thought we were going to make decorations," I finally told Mindy, after I had to chase after the third runaway ball. Carolyn and Tracy just stood there whenever the ball rolled away. I motioned Mindy over to the side. "We'll never be finished by Friday." We still had to go over to the A & P market and find some big cardboard boxes to make tombstones for everyone to sit on.

"You go ahead," she said, and then she went tearing back to the group while I stood staring stupidly after her.

10 ≋ "Welcome to the House of Horrors"

The day of the party dawned dismal and rainy. The bleak sky hovered menacingly over the buildings, and the clouds moved in dark swirls across the sky. A perfect day for a Monster Bash! I couldn't wait to go over to Carolyn's house. We had practically bought out Mr. Newton's Novelty Nook for cardboard skeletons to hang in the closets, monster masks, and gauze-like witches to fly from the rafters of Carolyn's spooky attic, turned over for us to transform by her dubious parents. Carolyn, Tracy, and I had ended up doing most of the work after school every afternoon. Mindy said she had piano lessons, doctor's appointments, or unexpected errands. When I complained to the others, they didn't respond. Maybe I should have kept my mouth shut.

We had fun anyway, cutting out old horror-tale comic books and pasting them on poster paper for place-mats. Mindy was there that morning when I arrived at

Carolyn's. WELCOME TO THE HOUSE OF HORRORS was painted in red, dripping letters on the wall.

"I wasn't sure you were going to show up," Mindy said, putting the finishing touches on the sign. "You're so late." I resisted the impulse to ask her where she'd been all week.

"Listen to this," said Tracy. She turned on a tape recording of organ music. The slow funeral-like sounds penetrated the room.

"Perfect," I said, letting the music put me in the mood. We spent the day making sinister signs: THIS WAY TO THE TORTURE CHAMBER, BEWARE OF THE WEREWOLF, SNAKE PITS, PRIVATE PARTY—NO MORTALS ALLOWED. Tracy and I stuffed old clothes with newspapers and hung them around. "Special guests," I said, giving them extra insulation in the tummy. The figures bobbed headless and spooky from hooks stuck in the walls.

Around lunchtime, I hinted that perhaps the time had come to create our feast fit for a beast.

"A Draculuscious banquet," sang Tracy as we slid down the banister into the kitchen.

Munching on peanut-butter-and-jelly sandwiches, we pulled out Carolyn's punchbowl and began mixing the gruesome ingredients for Poisonous Purple Punch, a recipe taken out of Lorna's *Dynamite Party Book*:

> 2 quarts ginger ale
> 4 six-ounce cans frozen grape juice
> 2 pints lime sherbet
> 2 pints raspberry sherbet

Bowls of ice cream, served with chocolate chips, sliced bananas, coconut, chocolate syrup, crushed pineapple, whipped cream, nuts, red hots, marshmallow topping, gum drops, pretzel sticks, and raisins completed the menu.

"This will be the gloppiest, bloppiest sundae ever created," I said, rubbing my hands together and rolling my eyes around devilishly. I was already drooling. Dinner the night before had consisted of a dried-out lamb chop and overcooked broccoli. I was starving!

We spent the rest of the afternoon planning games and putting out makeup for everyone to create monster faces.

At 3:00, Mindy and I went back to her apartment to fill some suitcases with Natasha's old outfits for a dress-up game. The closet was stuffed with boots of every color, wigs, hats with plumes, ribbons, and beads, and an assortment of long dresses that could have been ordered right out of a Frederick's of Hollywood catalogue. I wondered why Natasha needed a short, blond, curly wig, but I didn't ask Mindy.

Carl happened to walk in as I was pulling a lacy black dress over my head. He smiled widely and whistled. I grinned back at him through the netting. Mindy said, "Get out. You're embarrassing my friend."

"No," I sputtered, more embarrassed by Mindy's nastiness. "Please stay. Umm, have you won any chili contests lately?"

"As a matter of fact," said Carl, "that's why I came over. To show my kids this trophy." From behind his back he produced a large gold cup. Engraved on the bottom were the words *First Prize Skokie Chili Cook-off*.

"Congratulations," I said as I shook his freckled hand.

Then Carl and I had a long discussion about the advantages of green peppers as opposed to red peppers, scallions instead of yellow onions, and chunks of beef rather than ground chuck. His cheeks became flushed as he talked animatedly. I definitely wanted to take him home to meet Mother. If anyone could convince her of the joys of cooking, it would be Carl.

Mindy sat watching us silently, her arms folded stiffly on her stomach. The madder she looked, the more fun I had talking to Carl. Just because she was nasty to her dad didn't mean I had to be. Besides, I really liked him, with his funny, mismatched clothes and his sad-clown face. He just needed someone to give him a big hug. Then Lorna appeared at the door and they gave each other "isn't he hopeless" looks. I realized that Mindy was copying Lorna's attitudes toward Carl, and that in some way they both blamed him for having to move into the apartment and change schools.

When he left the room, Mindy said, "What a jerk!"

"Your dad's really nice. Why are you so terrible to him?" I knew by the way she looked over at me that we were going to have a fight. I continued boldly, "He tries so hard. He just wants to please you, to make you smile . . . that's why he's always saying funny things." I was rambling on now, afraid to stop, afraid to go on. I held in check my other angry feelings about Mindy and concentrated on her and Carl. If I could just get this far, if she would just listen and understand, maybe I could tell her the rest of my grievances later.

Mindy sat there expressionless, although her eyes narrowed a bit. "Well, anyway," I finally ended my tirade, "I think he's nice, and he is your father."

Mindy said, "Why don't you just stay out of it. Just mind your own business. Just because you live in a big house and your father has all that money, you think you know everything."

"That's not true," I yelled. "You can't say that. You're always bossing me around. And you always have to have everything your way. Well, your way . . ." I was stammering and stuttering now. All the things I had held back came blurting out ". . . your way isn't fair and I'm sick of it. Why can't you listen to someone else for a change?"

Mindy thrust her chin forward. "Oh, fine," she said. "You can say that all you want, but no one will agree with you."

"That's what you think. Everyone knows how mean you are and you know it, too!"

"We'll see about that," said Mindy. Cool as an icicle, she glided out of the room. After sitting there for a few minutes, I stood up, opened the front door quietly, and went home.

I slipped in the back door. Jill was making a sandwich out of lettuce, crackers, and the last slice of American cheese. Mother was reading, her glasses nodding from their shaky perch on her nose. I sat down and waited for them to topple off. She finally looked over at me and slid them back over her forehead.

"Yes, Anabeth?"

"If you think a friend is doing something wrong," I said slowly, "would you tell her?"

"I expect I would," said Mother, "if I felt it needed saying."

"But what if that friend didn't like to be criticized?"

"Most people only like criticism if it's unqualified praise," Jill said.

Mother smiled sympathetically, but she didn't question me.

Jill said, "Just the other day I wrote in my quotation book something my social-studies teacher, Dr. Aldrich, said: 'Always have the confidence to speak your mind and the courage to stand behind your words.'" But in my case, I thought, speaking my mind is getting me into trouble.

Unconsciously, I poked my finger in the fishbowl. I let it hang there, feeling the cool water on my fingertip. Suddenly I felt a familiar tug like a quick kiss. One by one, each fish swam up, nipped my finger, and swam away. Then I was calling Mother over, jumping up and down . . . "They know me! The fish know me! They kissed my finger and it wasn't even dinnertime." My journal had been filling up with data. If the fish continued to nip my finger, food or no food, at any time of the day, I could validate my hunch that they were responsive fish. Jill's prediction that they were oblivious and Mrs. Rumplemeyer's warning would be proven wrong.

"Our 'Fish Tale' reports are going to be outstanding," announced Mother. "Good work, Anabeth."

11 ❧ The Monster Bash

"I'm off to the Monster Bash. I'll be home when the werewolf comes out, so don't bother to make a five-course meal tonight," I told Mother as I swept into the kitchen in her long, black-velvet cape.

"Don't worry, I won't," said Mother.

"Eat, drink, and be merry, for tomorrow you may diet," said Jill, opening the icebox and pointing to the empty shelves.

"I'll bring you home a melted Transylvania Treat," I told her. I thought about calling Mindy before I left for Carolyn's, but I figured that by now she had gotten over my outburst about Carl; at least I hoped she had. But that belligerent "We'll see about that" kept flashing on and off in my mind like a warning signal. Mindy was the first friend I had ever had who scared me. I remember in second grade, when Tracy's two front teeth were chipped, we all called her "Snaggle-tooth." She kept hiding behind the teacher's skirt and crying. I knew she was afraid and I pitied her for being so weak. Tracy still acts the same way. But now I was afraid, too.

Carolyn's house was all lit up. There were candles in every window. The sun was just going down and the sky was silvery pink after the spring shower. I pulled the cape tightly around my shoulders and prepared for my grand entrance. I leaped through the entrance hall and landed at the feet of Mr. and Mrs. Turner, who, still dubious, were reading off a list of rules to Carolyn, Tracy, and Mindy. No one acknowledged my presence. Were they ignoring me or just listening intently?

1. No running up and down the stairs, sliding down banisters, moving around in general.
2. No wandering outside after dark.
3. No kissing games.
4. No food throwing.
5. Use the bathroom on the third floor.
6. Everyone gone by ten o'clock.
7. Except Mindy, Anabeth, and Tracy, who stay to clean up.

"Of course. Absolutely." We all nodded indulgently at them. Mrs. Turner unrolled a long piece of plastic over the furniture in the living room. The pink velvet upholstered chairs peeked timidly out at us from under their see-through covering. Mrs. Turner eyed us timidly as well.

Then the doorbell started ringing . . . kids thronged through the doors. The Turners disappeared into their bedroom and turned the TV up. I counted three Count

Draculas, a witch, two mummies, five vampires, one King Kong, two ghosts, a Frankenstein, two monsters, a Wolfman, and seven Blobs. I noticed Rachel didn't show up. We blindfolded everyone and led them upstairs. The spooky organ music droned forebodingly in the background. Just like Halloween, I thought. Six pots arranged in a line gleamed repulsively at the top of the stairs.

"Take off your shoes and socks and stand in a circle," screeched Mindy, her face painted white, slinky in Natasha's red, silky negligee. We began to pass the pots from person to person.

"You are lost in Dracula's dungeon and you must feel your way out," continued Tracy in a low, wheedling tone.

"Eyeballs," I announced, sticking Neil's hand in the pot of peeled grapes. Then I shoved his foot in the cold spaghetti. "Worms!" he yelped. Soon everyone's hands squished around in raw eggs for guts, dried apricots for ears, corncobs for bones, and finally, soapy water for acid. We turned up the organ music to drown out the howling. When we switched the lights back on and pulled down the blindfolds, there was a mad dash for the bathroom and paper towels.

Just as I was about to reach down to pick up the pot of spaghetti to pitch out, I felt a hard shove on my back. Slipping on a slimy lump of pasta, I tripped and ended up in a puddle of soapy water, spaghetti, and grapes. The velvet cape emerged a soggy mess. I looked up to find Mindy laughing at me. Some of the others were laughing, too. I pretended it was all a big joke, even though I knew she had purposely pushed me. I started to throw a handful of eyeballs at her, when Tracy screamed, "Remember the rules. Do you want Carolyn's parents to come running up here?"

"She started it," I grumbled, shaking the goo off and standing up. Mindy gave me the sneer that I had become so familiar with and went off, whispering to Tracy.

When Mindy divided us into two teams for the dress-up relay, she didn't include me. I edged away from the group. If the others noticed that I had been pushed out, they didn't show any sign. I started cleaning up the pots, pretending that I was busy. Tracy, Carolyn, and Mindy organized the rest of the games and announced the refreshments as if I weren't even there, as if I had had nothing to do with the party. We played Monster Telephone, put on makeup, invented monster tongue twisters and a host of other monster-maddening, spine-tingling, rib-tickling games that I vaguely participated in. I went through the motions of laughing and joking, but inside I was aware of only two facts: Mindy was furious, and I was scared. Did the other kids know? Did they care? Every time I approached her, she turned away in an angry huff. "What's wrong? What's wrong?" I wanted to ask. What did I do that was so terrible? Carolyn and Tracy looked over at me a few times in apprehensive silence. I didn't even stay to clean up. I wanted to avoid a confrontation with Mindy. I knew Carolyn and Tracy would be on her side. Neil's dad drove me home. I don't remember saying thank you or good night. I don't remember undressing or getting into bed. But I do remember the dreams. Huge, white-faced monsters dressed in red, storming and raging in and out of a dark attic. They towered over me. Their voices, dark and thundering, accused. "Traitor! Coward!" they repeated over and over again. Then Rachel's face appeared, her eyes round and luminous. I reached out for her. She faded into the blackness. I woke in a sweat, my heart beating loudly. I could not fall asleep again, so I scribbled nonsensical words on my note pad until daybreak. Then I dozed off again.

"Anabeth, it's almost noon. Wake up. The telephone's for you." Mother was calling up the stairs.

I felt as if I had taken too much cold medicine. My head hurt as I dragged myself out of bed. Mindy's voice was loud and cross over the phone. "How come you didn't stay to clean up?"

"I don't know," I stammered. "I didn't think you wanted me to, the way you were acting."

"Well, I'm over at Carolyn's with Tracy. We're cleaning up for you, Miss Rich Bitch." Then she hung up. I felt as if I had stepped into quicksand and was being pulled under. Now Mindy would have something else to hold against me.

When I wandered into the kitchen to rustle up some cornflakes, Mother, Jill, and Dad were all standing there, waiting for me. I wondered how they knew about what had happened. They had strange expressions. All I could think of to say was "Hi."

"You'd better tell her," Jill said to Mother.

"Tell me what?" I asked, irritated to find an empty box of cereal.

"Anabeth," said Dad very gently, "this morning when

we came in for breakfast, we found Goggles and Shabun-kin on the counter. They must have flipped over the top during the night."

Mother broke in, "I probably filled the bowl with too much water."

"What? What did you say?" I was having a hard time registering the words.

"We can go to Mrs. Rumplemeyer's later and buy two more fish if you want. I'm so sorry," Mother said.

I started to tremble. "I don't want any more fish. I just don't care. Why isn't there ever any food around here?" I screamed, hurling the empty box of cornflakes on the floor.

I spent the afternoon in my room. I thought about the "Iceberg and Its Shadow" and wished I were back at the museum, moving through those cool, clear passageways. I thought about Rachel and how hurt and defenseless she must have been feeling. I had really let her down. I wanted to call her, but knew it was too late. I should have called her weeks ago. Then I think I fell asleep again.

I dreamed I was lost in a palace made of ice. Propelled onward by a moving shadow, I followed the dark shape in and out of labyrinths that had no end. The air became colder and colder. At last I reached a high wall. It had no door. I called and called. My voice echoed through the ice cavern. No one answered. I beat my fists hard against the frozen surface. When it cracked, I found myself staring into a huge mirror, and my reflection was only a shadow. I woke up shivering.

12 ❧ "Today my tears filled up a fishbowl"

School became pure torture for me. One morning my desk was moved out of the circle into a corner. Mindy, Carolyn, and Tracy renamed themselves the Three Musketeers. Rachel, who was still sitting with Lonnie Nuell, didn't seem to react to these new developments one way or the other. I was sure she saw what was going on. You're probably glad I'm being ostracized, I wanted to tell her. Yet I could hardly blame her for steering clear of me. What had I done when she was in trouble? Now we were treating each other like strangers. And no one else wanted to have anything to do with me, either.

With a passion, I devoted myself to my math workbook. Twice my books were cleared out of my desk while I was at gym. I found them stuffed into the empty aquarium under the bookshelves, reminding me of my dead fish and making me feel even worse. I began hanging on the edge of Mindy's group, hoping they would change their minds.

"Get away! Stop following us around," Mindy told me.

"What did I do?" I kept asking, and hating myself for needing to. Each time I tried to placate her, I felt as if a part of me was disappearing.

"You're not a loyal friend," snarled Mindy. "Look what you did to Rachel, and I heard what you said about me."

How did she manage to turn everything around? She was the one who had started it. No matter what I said or did, I couldn't compete with her. She was too strong for me. I felt weak, as if I were shrinking or becoming invisible. And no one would stick up for me. Even Neil stopped tagging after me. If I tried to talk with any of the other girls, Mindy would motion them over, and then I would be alone again. When I brought my photographs from Disney World to hang on the bulletin board, Mindy said, "You think you're so great just because you live in a big house and go on a lot of vacations."

Were they jealous of me because the boys liked me, because they thought I was rich? But I couldn't think of one time that I had ever acted conceited or showed off. I wasn't like Cathy Rose, in the fifth grade, who always wore a rabbit-fur coat to school and had five-dollar bills stuffed in her desk. Whenever anyone blew up at her, she would give one away. I knew I wasn't like her.

One day Mrs. Trilling asked me what was wrong. I seemed down in the dumps. I wasn't acting like my usual happy self.

"Nothing," I told her. "I'm having allergy problems, that's all."

"I know how you're feeling," she said in a tone that puzzled me. "I'm having my own problems." I wondered what she meant.

"What's the matter? What's the matter with Teacher's Pet?" Tracy mimicked later. Then she put her hand over her mouth and giggled. I used to like her giggle. But now it sounded nasty to me.

I ate my tuna sandwich, potato chips, and Snickers bar alone and went right home after school. Mother and Jill were sitting at the table examining the contents of a large white folder.

"Two months! A chance of a lifetime! I'm so excited for you," Mother was saying. Both Mother and Jill were clearly elated. Jill waved a paper at me.

"Look," she said, "I've been accepted by the Experiment in International Living to go to France. Three weeks living with a French family and then biking through the Loire Valley."

"That's wonderful, Jill," I said, trying to muster up some warmth in my tone. I suppose it should be a compliment to me that my older sister was such a success, but today I was having a difficult time feeling very pleased. In fact, I was uneasy, anxious to get away from her.

"And you should congratulate me, too," Mother said. "I'm the new research assistant for Dr. Tobias, the Dean of the School of Social Work. My appointment came today. There's going to be a social worker in the family."

I looked at their shining faces, my mother and sister glowing with energy, absorbed in their new projects.

Here I was with no friends and no fish. Anabeth Blair, not much good at anything. I turned around and left the room. I heard Jill exclaim, "What's her problem?"

"I'm not sure," answered Mother, "but she sure hasn't been herself lately. She goes straight to her room after school. I don't even have to tell her not to tie up the phone. Maybe it has to do with the fish."

"The fish," I muttered to myself. "That's the least of my worries."

Later that night, after a cup of Mother's watery chicken soup and a toasted cheese sandwich, I sat on the stool at the counter, staring at my one remaining fish. Goldy seemed as lonely as I. She nipped my finger each time I dipped it in the bowl. I wanted to kiss her back. I felt the pressure building up between my eyes as I watched the tears drip down from my cheeks into the water. Goldy jerked as if to ask, "What was that?"

Then I took the pencil and started writing in my journal.

> Today, my tears have filled up a fishbowl.
> The fish welcomes them,
> Puckering her lips to cheer,
> Flicking her tail with joy.
> She thinks she needs my tears,
> But what do fish know about sorrow?
>
> Sometimes, it seems I cry for no reason at all,
> Feeling the tears well up, spill down my cheeks,
> My nose running, blending salt flavors on my lips,
> My face puffy, contorted,
> The sheer sobbing joy of it.
> I even flood the basement.

The bathtub overflows with my tears,
And the floor becomes hysterical.
You don't know that about me,
Do you?
The fish, my golden fish knows,
And she doesn't seem to mind.

That night, when I crawled into bed, I lay there afraid to close my eyes. Too many strange demons had appeared in my dreams lately. I saw Mother standing at my doorway.

"Anabeth," she said, "are you all right?" I didn't answer. She came to the head of the bed and bent down to kiss me good night. She hadn't done that in a long time. She put her cheek next to mine. I liked the soft feeling and the smell of scented cream that she uses at night. "I love you, Anabeth," she whispered.

"Me, too." Then she tiptoed out.

The demons stayed away that night.

The next morning I was certain my nose was playing tricks on me. I smelled bacon frying, freshly baked biscuits, and cinnamon. Throwing on my terry-cloth bathrobe, I hurried down to check out the kitchen. A flurry of activity was going on. Jill was setting the table and Mother was putting strawberry marmalade into a silver container. My favorite. Dad was mixing a batch of scrambled eggs.

"Surprise," called Mother when she saw me, a bewildered grin on my face. "We decided to raid the supermarket and prepare a feast."

"You and Jill are celebrating?"

"Partly," she said, "but mostly, I wanted to surprise you with something special."

"And hopefully, this begins a new reign in this household," exclaimed Dad, "of gourmet meals with spices from India, puffed pastry à la Julia Child, beef bourguignon, and baked Alaska."

"Don't get carried away." Mother laughed.

"The cupboard will no longer be bare," said Jill. She glanced quickly at my journal on the counter. Then I understood. They were really nice, my family. Trying to cheer me up. My eyes began to fill up and my nose felt stuffy.

"Come on, Princess," said Dad, scooping me up in his arms and depositing me on a chair. "You're going to be the first one fed."

The biscuits were steaming hot, dripping with butter, and the eggs just the way I liked them, a little runny with lots of pepper. Mother even squeezed fresh orange juice. I gobbled up my food faster than she could serve it. A dozen eggs and a pound of bacon later, we all sat back in our seats, completely satiated.

"That was the best meal we've had in weeks," said Dad, rubbing his stomach.

"My compliments to the chefs," I said. There was a momentary pause, and then Mother was watching me carefully.

"Anabeth, do you want to tell us what's been bothering you lately? We'd like to help if we can."

I nodded, relieved. I felt as if I'd been carrying a heavy weight on my shoulders. Once I started, I couldn't stop. I began at the beginning with Rachel, and then told them about Mindy, Carl, the Monster Bash, and school. By the time I finished, I was sobbing. Dad handed me his clean white handkerchief. I blew my nose.

Mother, Dad, and Jill began talking at once.

"Those little brats," said Jill.

"Why, that's the worst. I'm shocked. Anabeth has always been so well liked. I can't understand it," from my mother.

"Let's look at this logically," offered Dad.

"Why don't you call Rachel?" suggested Mother. "Tell her how you feel."

"I can't," I said. "She won't believe me now."

Mother tried to convince me as I protested angrily, the tears starting to flow again.

"She can't right now," Jill interrupted. "Just drop that subject." And then Jill and Mother began arguing as if I weren't even there.

Jill blamed my problems on Mindy's sister, Lorna. "She's the biggest garbage mouth in the school, and Mindy gets her rotten personality from her."

"Mindy's family doesn't give her enough love, so she feels the rest of the world owes her something."

"She latched on to Anabeth and separated her from her friends so she could be the class leader."

"She's manipulative and disruptive because that's the only way she can get noticed."

"She needs acceptance so badly that she'll do anything to get it."

The amateur psychology went on and on.

"There's no figuring her out," I wanted to shout. "She's just a big, dumb lummox! A disgusting warthog!"

I knew I should appreciate the fact that my family was on my side, but I wished they would stop yapping about Mindy. The more they blamed her, the worse I felt. Was that because I knew nothing they could say or do would stop her? Even though I couldn't admit it to them, I realized that some of their criticism of Mindy could be directed at me, too. Some leader I turned out to be. I remembered when we first declared war on Rachel. I sat staring at the wall instead of speaking out for her. I remembered Rachel's face when they backed her up against the fence. I went on playing kickball and pretended not to notice. Now I was the one backed up to the wall. And somehow Mindy Gottfried, even with all her rotten, lowdown tricks, didn't come off as being the only villain.

Mother, indignant, dumbfounded, was talking as if the whole thing were happening to her instead of me. "I'm going to call Mrs. Trilling," she insisted. "I've never heard of such behavior."

"Don't do that," I begged. "You'll make everything worse. They'll just call me a tattletale." Breakfast was beginning to feel like a lump in my stomach. My family meant well, but I knew that they couldn't change what was already a chilling fact. I was an outcast for the first time in my life.

Dad looked over at me. "I have to go downtown for a few hours," he said. "I know you feel badly right now, but you'll find an answer. It just takes time. The truth is that you discovered that Mindy isn't the kind of person that you want for a friend. She doesn't make you feel good about yourself. But it's hard to break away from her." He was right. At first, I loved all the attention from Mindy. I was flattered that she picked me. Yet she had a knack for making me feel uncomfortable . . . especially by the way she treated other people. Now I was the target. I wanted to make peace with her, but at the same time, I didn't like her, didn't want to be part of her group any more. I gave Dad a grateful kiss goodbye and left Mother and Jill still arguing. They were analyzing my problem as if it were a question on a chemistry exam, as if they could come up with a perfect solution.

In the afternoon, Mindy and Carolyn rode by on their bicycles. They circled around the block a few times and finally came up the driveway. I wondered what they wanted. Maybe they had decided to make up. I went outside and pretended to be going to the mailbox.

"We came by to pick up some clothes that I left here when I spent the night," said Mindy in a cold voice. She marched by me. I just stood there like a lump. Carolyn didn't say anything, didn't even look at me. I felt scared. I followed them inside. What else could I do? I tried to find some words to utter that wouldn't sound too foolish, but none presented themselves to me.

Mother saw their approach and cautiously nodded.

When they were out of sight, I warned, "Don't say anything. Stay out of it."

She was revving up for a confrontation. "They're in my house," she said, "and I don't like to see you so unhappy."

My two adversaries reappeared. Mother smiled at them. "Why don't you girls sit down and talk about what's troubling you," she said in an even tone. Mindy and Carolyn stopped in their tracks, two T-shirts and a pair of corduroys hanging limply over their arms. "Come on now," continued Mother smoothly, "do you think you're being fair to Anabeth? You girls have been good friends all year." This wasn't going to work.

"Please, Mother." I pleaded to no avail.

"Carolyn," Mother said, making a last attempt, "I've known you since you first moved to Skokie. We all used to go up to the 8th Street playground together. Now I'll just leave and let the three of you talk." She swept out, a hopeful smile on her face.

I moved the papers on the counter around in rapid hopelessness. "Do you want a soda?" My voice sounded strained and meek.

"We have to go," said Mindy curtly. "I guess the next thing you'll do is have your mother call the school." She gave a short laugh.

"Let's go. Come on, Mindy," said Carolyn, who still couldn't look me in the eye. Why had Carolyn changed so much toward me? I thought sadly. We used to be such good friends. As they rode past our greenhouse, I remembered the times Carolyn and I had made mud pies there, had grown tomatoes from seeds together. Soon their bikes disappeared into the green and blue of the first really warm day of the spring. I briefly noted the dogwoods now bursting white on our lane. I watched the empty street dully.

Mother returned. "Well, did that work?" she asked cheerfully.

"Yes," I answered her in the strongest voice I could muster. "Yes, it sure did." To my surprise, she seemed to believe me and began humming happily to herself.

I worked on my fish report for a while. After that, I wrote about the white dogwoods and tried to push from my mind any thoughts of what would be waiting for me at school on Monday.

13 ≈ "Stop the world, I want to get back on"

I began counting the days until the end of school, marking them off on my calendar, with a sense of grim satisfaction at the accumulation of red X's. I would be awarded summer vacation as a consolation prize. I would sit on a rock at the beach writing poems. I would bicycle over to my cousin's in Forest Park. I would help my grandmother with her garden. But I wouldn't have to see anyone from Skokie Elementary School until September. There was nothing much else to do but wait for June and grin and bear it. I ignored Mother's questioning glances and kept my problems to myself. There was no telling how she would react if I told her that Mindy had launched a Mama's Baby campaign. It was one of those nicknames that others in the class picked up easily. No one said it out loud in front of Mrs. Trilling, but they would mouth it when she had her back to us. I learned when to avert my eyes and when to sidestep legs and arms that would flash out as I passed. When the Three Musketeers weren't looking, I would study each of them and mark down notes in my journal.

Carolyn: Clumsy, with an Adam's apple that moves faster than her mouth, long neck, fat rear end, knock knees, a giraffe (belongs in the zoo).

Tracy: Tiny, with squinty eyes, pointy ears, squeaky voice, a mouse (common household variety).

Mindy: Straggly, disheveled black mane, flaring nostrils, long, bony legs, buck teeth, a farm horse (ready for the glue factory).

My other preoccupation, which lacked that sneaky "eye for an eye, tooth for a tooth" quality but was certainly more productive, involved putting together my report and planning the class activity.

One evening we spread all our notes out on the table and began organizing them in sections.

"You need to have an outline, too," I told Mother.

"This is the first time we've had a pet in the house that hasn't been ignored after a week," she said. "And you also managed to prove your hypothesis. What's your secret?"

"Conditioning," I said.

"I'm sure Professor Tobias will laugh when I suggest a research grant to test out your theory—I can see it now —a whole crew of eager clinicians, fingers poised over fishbowls."

The next morning everyone came to school prepared to give their reports, except Mindy, who claimed that she certainly hadn't forgotten but her paper had been mistakenly thrown out with the trash, and anyway, her hamster, Murgatroyd, refused to cooperate and do anything particularly worth writing about. A series of disasters about which she was truly crushed. Mrs. Trilling said, "Have it on my desk tomorrow or else."

I was nervous about my turn. I figured that no one would want to participate in my class activity. I had been up until midnight laboring over the cover. I could have used Rachel's help with the intricate design. The kids will probably start calling me Fish Freak instead of Mama's Baby, I thought to myself as I approached the front of the class. My head was pounding. I felt a wave of nausea and my right knee was bouncing up and down. I stared out at the sea of blank faces. I began telling them about our family's bad luck with pets, Mrs. Rumplemeyer's warning, and Goggles and Shabunkin flipping over the side.

"Sounds fishy to me," Neil called out. There were a few titters. I plunged onward.

"Since my report is entitled 'A Fish Tale,' " I said, "I would like you all to join me in making up a fishy story right here." I directed the group to form a circle. Then I whispered a secret word in everyone's ear. All the words had something to do with fish. Aquarium, sand, ocean, shell. When I came to Mindy, she jerked back as if I were passing on a disease.

"The object of the game," I said, "is to disguise your word in a collective story. One person begins the story, and when he's ready, even if it's in the middle of a sentence, he passes it on to the next person until everyone's had a chance to tell part of the story. The last person in the circle must end the fish tale. Remember, there should be a beginning, middle, and end that makes sense. Then we'll try to guess each one's secret word." To my amazement, there were no protests. In fact, a general hum of enthusiasm greeted my plan.

"There was once a fisherman who lived in a house by the sea," began Tracy. She paused as if her imaginative powers stopped right there.

"That's a cinch," shouted Billy Moran. "Fisherman is her word."

"Wait until the end. Let the whole group have a turn before you start guessing," I said to Billy, careful not to let my tone imply that I was being bossy, careful not to reveal the shakiness that seemed to be lying at the edge of any statement I might make today. But Billy and the rest of the class, for that matter, accepted my direction easily, as if Mrs. Trilling herself had decreed it, and continued weaving an immensely illogical story about fishermen, pirates, mermaids, and sea dragons.

Rachel disguised her secret word "seashell" in an elaborate web of sea lore, a long series of fish-related words that, for a moment, stumped even me. I thought I detected a little smile cast briefly in my direction when she finished. No doubt about it, Rachel was the only one whose word the rest didn't catch on to immediately. And more importantly, my project was a success. I finished my report by reading a poem that even Mother insisted on copying for herself.

> *Probable. Possible, my goldfish*
> *Nips my finger with a Relative swish,*
> *It can't be explained in the Positive now,*
> *Because I'm unable to Postulate how.*

A little scattered applause and a mumbling of "That was good" and I was on my way down the aisle back to my seat. Mrs. Trilling said, "I hope the rest of the reports are as entertaining and well worked out as yours, Anabeth. And I'd love to borrow your poem for the bulletin board."

"Bring the fish to school," said Robin Skylar. "I want to see her swim up and nip your finger."

"Yeah, bring the little nipper."

"Okay." I nodded, basking in the glory of the first nice words anyone outside my family had said to me for weeks.

My report was followed by dog stories, cat tales, ant-farm experiments, canary, parrot, and cockatoo narrations, spider, cockroach, and wasp investigations, gerbil and hamster accounts, and finally, Neil Bennet's lengthy description of his pet boa constrictor, Julius Squeezer.

At lunch, as I prepared to unwrap my tuna sandwich, Neil sat down next to me.

"I think Julius can be tamed, too," he announced. "I have the whole plan worked out. First I ring a bell, then I serve his dinner." The idea, according to Neil, was that Julius would begin to respond to the bell with or without the food.

"My suggestion is you should leave Julius alone and find a friendly garter snake."

"That's no challenge," Neil said. "Hey, do you want to come by my house and see him?" That was probably the last thing I wanted to do, but for the sake of keeping the conversation going at least until I finished my Twinkie, I said, "Sure."

Pretty soon Billy and Robin joined in, and we generally agreed that as pets go, a boa constrictor was not ideal.

"My mother says that if I have unusual hobbies like raising boa constrictors or alligators, I have a better chance of getting into Harvard," insisted Neil.

Mindy minced over to the table. She assumed an icy pose. "Is Mama's Baby hanging around with the boys?"

Instead of shrinking back the way I usually did, I said, "Neil, I know a great place to set Julius loose." They all roared. Mindy's nostrils flared, but she didn't respond. I didn't care what she thought or said any more.

We trudged back to class for the last set of reports. Mrs. Trilling was standing by the window. When she saw us, she wiped her eyes with a handkerchief and went to her desk. Her face was very pale. By the time everyone had assembled, she had composed herself. She stood up and said in a very calm voice, "Boys and girls, I want to make an announcement that makes me very sad." She stepped toward us a few paces and I could tell by the way she was wringing her hands together that whatever Mrs. Trilling was about to say was as hard for her as presenting my report had been for me. "This will be my last year at Skokie Elementary. I was informed by Dr. Munch today that my contract will not be renewed."

There were a few murmurings, but most of us were quiet, caught off guard.

"I want you to know that you have been a wonderful group, and I've loved working with you. I think we've all learned a lot, including me. I just wanted you to know why I'm so upset." I could have asked her so many questions, but the lump in my throat was turning into a watermelon. "I think that your parents will be pleased to find out that all of you improved your scores on the reading achievement tests," she continued. "Although your spelling and grammar were low, that can easily be raised with a little extra effort. But your vocabulary is the best in the district." Then she paused as if on the verge of another disclosure, but instead said, "Let's turn to page 67 in your social-studies reader. We'll continue the reports tomorrow."

The afternoon passed in a blur. I knew now why Mrs. Trilling had understood so well my "allergy" problems of the last few weeks. I was allergic to Mindy Gottfried and she was having an allergic reaction to Dr. Munch. I had an urge to tramp down to Dr. Munch's office, throw open the door, and demand a retraction. When the dismissal bell rang, I went over to Mrs. Trilling and gave her a big hug. Her long arms tightened around me and then she said, "Anabeth, you did very well today. I'm proud of you."

I bit my lip to hold back the tears. "Don't you worry. Everything will be fine," she said. I wanted to thank her for the "Iceberg and Its Shadow," for the poems, for helping me to notice the white dogwoods and the spiderweb. But there were too many people standing around. When Tracy hissed "Teacher's Pet," I didn't even care.

I ran all the way home. The sky was hazy and cloudy, but somewhere, too bright to be seen directly, the sun was blazing through. I felt the heat on my back and let my ponytail flap around my ears as I ran. I felt angry, the kind of angry that makes people want to shout and run and shove, instead of the angry I had been feeling for weeks, which chased me to my room, my notebooks, and my silent thoughts. I knew that if I didn't take a stand now, I never would. I also knew that even if I failed, at least I could say that I fought back, that I didn't slip into my shell like a turtle again. I felt some of my own power returning. Now I was ready for action.

I raced up my driveway and flung open the screen door. "Stop the world," I shouted, "I want to get back on."

Mother was bent over the sink chopping chunks of meat and onions. "Carl Gottfried sent me his prize-winning Chili con Carne Cockamamie recipe. It arrived in the mail today. He said you would understand."

"Carl's a nice man," I said. "He just has lousy taste when it comes to relatives."

"You can choose your friends, but you can't pick your relatives" came Jill's voice from the next room.

"Here, let me help you." I began peeling the tomatoes and dropping them in the big iron pot on the stove.

Mother and I finished making Carl's chili together, and I told her what had happened in school. I watched her expression change from a smile of satisfaction at my Fish Tale, to a concerned grimace.

"Sometimes, I think education is the last thing the school administrators are interested in," she said. "But what can we do about Mrs. Trilling?"

Then I told her about a plan that had been simmering in the back of my mind, a plan that was ready to boil over.

"All you can do is try," she said. "Dad and I are behind you."

That night I dreamed that I was standing on the edge

of a rocky cliff overlooking the ocean. Big black rocks began to rise from the sea and hurl themselves toward me. I became frightened as the dark shapes moved closer; but, as if I possessed a strange power, I reached out my arms to cast a spell on them—the rocks moved back to the sea and disappeared into the murky water.

When I woke up the next morning, I thought of Merlin the Magician, King Arthur's tutor, and how he was able to perform magical feats. In my dream, I had been just like Merlin. Maybe that was a good omen.

14 ⚘ "To whom it may concern..."

Cutouts of red apples, green trees, and circus animals are pasted to the windows of Skokie Elementary School. The building is clumsy, rambling, two stories, with not one inch of wasted space. Dr. Munch likes to tell us on assembly days, in the stuffy, crowded gymnasium, as parents sit stiffly on folding chairs in the rear, that "our school is bustling with activity. No, sir, not one inch of wasted space."

Maybe there's no wasted space at Skokie Elementary School, but we sure waste a lot of time. And time moves slowly here; at least it has for most of the seven years that I've been going in and out through the stone arch, advancing from the first to the second floor by virtue of age and a few points on the achievement tests.

This was what I was thinking as I walked toward the stone arch again, for the one thousandth time, the next morning. I was also thinking that sixth grade with Mrs. Trilling wasn't a waste of time, and I hoped the rest of the class would agree with me, too.

Mindy, Carolyn, and Tracy were blocking the arch. They pretended not to notice me. "May I get by?" I asked. "Big baboons," I added, to myself.

Mindy said, still ignoring me, "We're getting rid of Terrible Trilling. I bet Teacher's Pet cried all night."

"Excuse me," I tried again.

Four elbows were locked together. Their T-shirts, which read THREE MUSKETEERS in red, confronted me like billboards. Their faces told me it was no use talking to them any more.

I turned on my heel and ran down to the basement entrance. Why did they hate me so much? Why had Tracy and Carolyn, who used to be my friends, turn against me? As I pictured their gloating, ornery faces, I realized that they really believed I had let them down, that I had betrayed them. I guess I had been so involved with Rachel and then Mindy that they felt left out. Second-best. When we ganged up on Rachel, we were all thinking, I'm glad it's not me. Well, it's you now, said the little voice inside my head.

I had been mulling over what happened for weeks, playing it out in my mind a hundred times. I couldn't turn back the clock or erase what I did to Rachel like wiping chalk off a blackboard. And I couldn't bring myself to walk right up to her and say I'm sorry, either, even though part of me wanted to and I knew I should. First I needed to stop skulking around like a reject and feeling sorry for myself, to stand up to the Warthog and Company and do something worthwhile.

But I was feeling jittery and worried that my plan would never work. They'll ruin it, I thought. How can I even try?

The morning was long and boring, but at least I was able to sit back and tune out while the rest of the reports droned on. No one else had activities planned until Rachel. It was as if she and I had been the only ones who remembered. She did a report on two white mice, which she brought along in a Plexiglas cage. Then she placed boxes of acorns and leaves she had collected, white and black paper, scissors, and paste on the low worktable. She spread out a long sheet of brown wrapping paper on the floor.

She began her instructions in her low, shy voice. She was almost whispering, as the room became very quiet so we could hear what she was saying. "Please find a spot on the floor around the paper," she said. "Using the materials on the table, I want you to make a collage—a kind of natural mouse house—a place where the white mice could live and be happy."

Then she handed everyone a cut-out, white paper mouse to paste on the paper. Some were crouching or standing, sleeping or ready to run. We worked until it was time for lunch—cutting, pasting, building, out of leaves and acorns, a wonderful mouse kingdom. Even when the bell rang at noon, some of us were still working. We hung the completed mural out in the corridor.

I smiled at Rachel. She smiled faintly back at me. I wished so much that we were best friends again.

Siskiyou County
School Library

I walked slowly down to the cafeteria. My heart was thudding as if I had just run around the playground three times without stopping.

The class had agreed on my last plan, *The Skokie Scuttlebutt*, and then I had abandoned it in favor of Mindy's kickball games. Now they might think I'll give up on this one, too. I was afraid that the minute I opened my mouth they would all chant, "Teacher's Pet." Every step I took felt awkward and shaky, but I was determined not to let them know how much their hostility bothered me. I held my head so high that I could feel the stiffness all the way down my back. I took a deep breath and scanned the room. Mrs. Trilling wasn't there. I tapped on my glass with a spoon. "Everybody, I have an announcement."

Some people looked up. The Three Musketeers began to talk in loud voices.

"Please listen," I tried again. I could hear my voice cracking. I almost wanted to stop, but my mind raced on and my voice followed. I produced a sheet of white paper. "I care about Mrs. Trilling," I said, "and I don't want her to lose her job." Everyone was silent now, peering at me. "Maybe if we sign a petition to be sent to Dr. Munch and the superintendent, they will know how much we learned from Mrs. Trilling, how much we like her. Maybe then she won't lose her job."

"What does the petition say?" asked George suspiciously.

"To whom it may concern," I read in a clear, now steady voice. "This is to certify that the students of Mrs. Trilling's sixth-grade class protest your recent action regarding her. Not only is she a creative teacher, but she also understands kids and how to make us excited about learning."

Mindy said, "You're just trying to get attention for yourself. That's a dumb petition. We don't care about Terrible Trilling anyway." When she stalked off, Tracy and Carolyn trailed out behind her. I saw a few of the others begin to turn away.

I almost crumpled the paper up in my hands. I felt helpless, invisible again. But then Rachel yelled out, "I'd like to sign. I care about Mrs. Trilling. I don't think it's fair, either."

"Me, too," said Lonnie Nuell.

Then some of the boys circled around us. Everyone was pulling out their pencils, discussing the petition, trying to figure out if it would make a difference.

"Kid Power," announced Neil. "Let's get our parents to sign the petition, too."

By the end of the day, everyone in the sixth grade had put their signatures in the blank numbered spaces. Twenty-seven names. Everyone, that is, except Mindy, Tracy, and Carolyn.

I waited for Rachel on the steps after school. I wanted to thank her for making the first move to sign Mrs. Trilling's petition. But she came out with Lonnie and I was afraid to butt in. As usual, there was no one to walk home with, but this time I didn't mind as much. I had spoken out for someone else, someone who needed me to stand up for her. And for a time, I stopped worrying about myself. Whether the others still hated me or not, they had agreed with my plan. For the first time in days I felt happy —alone, but not lonely. I held the petition tightly in my hand as I ran through the tunnel under the railroad tracks. A train rumbled overhead as I shouted, "I did it! I really did it!" And when I heard the train's whistling toot, I felt as if it were cheering just for me.

15 ≈ "Here today and here tomorrow"

The day after school was over, I began complaining that I had nothing to do, no one to be with. Dad and I sat down and had a long talk.

"There are going to be times in your life, Anabeth, that you're going to have to learn to rely on yourself."

"I guess I have to figure out what I want to do." I was so used to being with friends all the time that hanging around the house seemed almost like a jail sentence.

"What's happened to you with your friends is sad. One day, you're on top of the world, and the next . . ."

". . . flat on my old wazoo," I said.

"I know that you feel hurt and rejected, but maybe you've learned something about what kind of people to choose for friends next time, about what it's like to be on the other side of the fence. Next year at junior high you'll meet a whole new group of girls."

"But I'm afraid Mindy's vendetta against me won't be

forgotten. Everybody knows her now. She's like an octopus with eight arms in every direction. I can't just start over. She'll turn the girls against me there, too." I was scared to go back to school in the fall. Even if I had three boring months ahead of me, at least I wouldn't have to be in school to face those mean looks every day.

"When school starts, you'll be surprised to find how many people are looking for new friends, trying to adjust to a big new school. You're going to have to be strong, to brave it out. Eventually the other girls will wise up, too."

But next fall seemed like a million years away. Dad might be right, but what good did that do me now? I felt discouraged. "I don't know when to be tough and when to give in."

Dad put his arms around me. "You'll know when the time comes," he said. "Look at what you accomplished this last week at school—the report, the petition. I'm proud of the way you've been handling a difficult situation."

"Thanks, Dad. I tried." Yet as mean as Mindy's maniacal mumblings were about me, in a strange way I missed her. I missed Tracy and Carolyn, too. But most of all I missed Rachel. Why was it so hard to let go?

"But who am I going to be with next year?" I moaned.

"Anabeth, the choice you don't know is the choice you can't make."

"Well, this time I'll do the choosing," I said with conviction.

"I believe you'll make the right choices, too," Dad said, pulling me close to him.

I could tell that Dad really did have faith in me. He

was convinced I could work my problem out. Mother had been giving me too many sad looks, and she kept talking to me in a soft voice. But at least she stopped bugging me to make plans, or asking me what I was doing every day.

A few days later, Jill announced that she heard Natasha and Seymour were getting married. I could picture them marching down the aisle in matching T-shirts.

"I ought to send them a wedding gift," remarked Mother.

"What were you thinking of?" I asked, surprised.

"Oh, maybe an exploding alarm clock."

"Just so the bomb goes off when the whole family's there," I said. We both laughed. I was glad we could finally joke about it.

That night we schlepped Jill to the airport to go to France. She had a knapsack strapped on her back and a duffel bag filled with French novels—even though she can't speak French yet.

As she boarded the plane, her last words to me were "Don't take life too seriously. We're here today and here tomorrow."

I hugged her very hard. "I hope by the end of the summer you'll be cured of your quotation mania," I said. *"Au revoir,"* she called. Mother and I watched until her plane disappeared.

The next day, I received a letter from Mrs. Trilling with three yellow goldfish printed on top. She said that she hadn't lost her job after all, that she was being transferred to the Skokie Experimental School, where the principal and the other teachers love music, poetry, and art. She was sure our petition helped. "I know you were responsible, Anabeth," she wrote. "And I thank you for your help."

Perhaps I'll finish my book of poems and send them to her. I'll write the dedication page to her. Maybe I'll even learn to cook (just in case Mother reverts back to her old habits).

I also knew the time had come for me to call Rachel, to tell her how sorry I was, how much I wanted to be her friend again. I wandered around the house a few times, cleaned out my desk, made a banana milk shake in the blender, and even washed my hair. I rehearsed what I should say. Rachel would probably be stubborn and hang up the first time. But I would call back. Then she would tell me how awful I was. "I'm really sorry," I'd say. "I know I've been a lousy friend. I'm a candidate for the Jerk of the Year award. But I miss you and want to be friends again." I practiced the last line about ten times in my head. I imagined us meeting at the corner holding up truce flags, or skywriting "I'm sorry," or even floating a bunch of red balloons over her house. My uncle proposed to my Aunt Helen over the ten o'clock news. About a hundred Helens telegrammed back YES to the station. Maybe Dad could rent a billboard or I could ride through the streets of Skokie in a mobile sound truck. "Rachel, I'm sorryeee" would echo all over town. Finally I picked up the telephone. My hand was shaking. The conversation went something like this:

ME: Hello, Rachel? This is Anabeth.
        Long pause.
RACHEL: Hi.
ME: What've you been doing?

118

RACHEL: Nothing much.

ME: Do you want to do something like come over or something?

Long pause.

RACHEL: I guess so.

ME: Really?

RACHEL: Sure.

ME: Hey, great! I'll meet you halfway at the fuchsia fireplug.

I hung up, filled with high hopes and a mounting feeling of uncertainty. How could I expect my friendship with Rachel to be the same? What should I say to her? Would we act natural or stand there eyeing each other like strangers? I reached for the phone again, then pulled my hand away. Maybe Rachel wouldn't ever trust me, but I knew I had to face her, to make amends, to show her that I cared. I wanted to take the risk and start at the end to find my way to a new beginning. Then I was out the door and on my way.

Siskiyou County Schools
LIBRARY
Property of
SISKIYOU COUNTY SUPT. OF SCHOOLS OFFICE